WHEN HOME FAILS

AN ESCAPE STORY OF A GROUP OF MIGRANTS TO AMERICA

DEMIAN W.

authorHOUSE®

AuthorHouse™
1663 Liberty Drive
Bloomington, IN 47403
www.authorhouse.com
Phone: 833-262-8899

Published by AuthorHouse   08/06/2021

ISBN: 978-1-6655-3419-2 (sc)
ISBN: 978-1-6655-3418-5 (hc)
ISBN: 978-1-6655-3420-8 (e)

Library of Congress Control Number: 2021915985

AUTHOR'S NOTE

A **S I WRITE** this story, a politician in power, somewhere, is living peacefully and lavishly in a mansion, carelessly creating policies that disfavor the "common," to further their own ambitions.

They are doing all but what they promised their citizens and threatening anyone who dares to question. Shame!

Meanwhile, to the good citizens of the world fleeing persecution of any kind, risking it all to get as far away from home as possible, be safe. You matter—and you are valuable.

CHAPTER 1

IT WAS ABOUT five in the morning in Mamfe, Cameroon. Endless gunshots thundered from afar as an old red Carina-E sped on the one-lane paved road, bypassing deserted villages and corpses barely covered with tree branches.

By the door, little Ella sat on the lap of her mother, who was crammed in the back seat among four other women. Two sizable men squeezed into the front seat next to the driver, making a total of eight in Tabi's vehicle, which was originally designed to carry five.

They approached the main entrance of the bridge linking Cameroon to Nigeria. A tall, slim, dark-skinned military officer stepped out of the bungalow positioned on the right side of the road. A bold sign over its front door read "Poste Frontière Cameroun Ekok" with the English translation beneath it in lowercase letters as if to announce the relative status of the two languages in the country.

He raised his right arm, bringing them to a slow halt. The name on his left chest pocket was Jean Pierre, and he was dressed in typical military style: a green beret, a camouflage army uniform over black leather boots, and a short gun that hung from the black belt fastening his neatly tucked shirt. The Cameroonian frontier had been operated by the immigration officers, but the recent deadly conflict in the country had forced its army to take over that duty.

Ella was watching through the side window as the officer approached the vehicle. His arrogance frightened her, and she buried her face in her mother's chest. She'd recognized something she did not want to see. At only seven, she had witnessed the military murder her father after burning their home in the village of Kwakwa, and she detested any sight that reminded her of that ordeal.

"Out!" he commanded in French, opening the right back door with a dreadful frown on his face.

As her mother struggled to exit the vehicle, Ella would not let go. She wrapped her arms around her mother's neck so tightly she nearly strangled her, and she locked her face into her mother's left shoulder, determined to remain there. She did not understand why her mother would bring her to this place, to encounter these people. The last time she saw this unforgettable uniform, the owners had left her fatherless and violated her fragile mind. Scarred it with images that will potentially haunt her for life. She was petrified.

Except for the driver, who remained seated, they all got out quietly with a pass in their hands, turned backward with their arms spread wide-open for scanning, and then proceeded into the building for pass inspections.

The inside of the immigration building was divided by plywood into five offices. Three were empty, and the other two were occupied by middle-aged military women. They each sat behind a glass counter, designed with a gap large enough for any documents to go through. It would have been busier if the war had not made traveling through the country nearly impossible, so that only the very brave and the rich dared to try.

Chefor, one of Tabi's passengers, felt as if he had been waiting at counter 2 forever. The three travelers who had trailed him into the building had proceeded to counter 1 and submitted their documents for clearance. It took each of them a maximum of three minutes to be evaluated and stamped out of Cameroon. The officer had looked at Chefor critically when he arrived and then picked up her phone and said nothing since then.

Is my countenance that unpleasant? I bet it's my eyes. I've always been told they are whiter than normal. Or is it my attire? Chefor mentally inspected himself. He wore a thick sky blue sweater over a pair of black jeans and sneakers. His haircut was typical of a twenty-four-year-old, though he seemed fatter than most guys that age. He stood there, staring in wonder and frustration at the woman who sat in the little office, going through her phone with a deep curiosity that made sense only to her, but why did she periodically examine his face and then resettle on her phone in utter disregard of his discomfort? He'd been standing there for about ten minutes unattended to when finally, she dropped her phone by the nameplate resting on the table before her. On it, was carved in bold, "Mrs. Chakunte," and she gazed straight into his eyes as though he had pissed her off.

"What are you going to do in Nigeria?" she asked in French, snatching the pass from the counter. Like most, if not all, military officers in Cameroon, she spoke only French, and she did so carelessly even when serving in a region of English speakers.

"I am going on a business trip, ma'am," Chefor replied in a steady voice, resolved to remain unaffected by the woman's inexplicable rudeness. He understood French but couldn't speak it, which was the case with some English-speaking Cameroonians.

She lifted her eyes from the piece of paper in her hand and looked at him distrustfully as though she knew he was lying.

Chefor's traveling companions were already cleared and heading through the side door that served as another entrance to the bridge from the immigration room. Ella was still glued to her mother's chest, and Tabi the driver was shutting the doors he'd opened for vetting. He then reentered his car as Jean Pierre proceeded to open the main gate that would allow him onto the bridge, which his passengers, except for Chefor, were now crossing by foot, heading toward the Nigerian immigration building that stood not too far away, at the end of the bridge.

"Where are you from?" she demanded authoritatively in French.

"Madam, I would love to continue with this unnecessary interrogation in Eng—"

"Where are you from?" she cut in, this time in pidgin English, with a coarse and deep voice Chefor thought a woman was not capable of.

But Mrs. Chakunte was one of a kind. There was a sophisticated virility to her that could rattle anyone. "Continue in English," she muttered, twisting her lips in provocation as she tried to mimic Chefor, but in a typically francophone Cameroonian English accent. "Why don't you speak French? Cameroon is a bilingual country," she affirmed.

A door creaked, and her colleague stepped out of her office with a phone and its charger. She then came into Mrs. Chakunte's office and plugged it in where an iPhone was charging. Perhaps the iPhone was Monsieur Jean's.

But why are they all charging their phones in someone else's office? Maybe theirs do not have a good power adaptor, Chefor thought.

The woman rushed out and appeared to speak with Monsieur Jean Pierre before she hastily walked away.

Over at Nigerian immigration, an overly friendly immigration officer seemed to have found joy in Ella's mother's company. "What kind of business are you in, my dear?" she asked, smiling and handing a pink lollipop to Ella, who stood by her mother more at ease than before, perhaps because the uniforms were now different, and the wearers were more jovial.

"Thank you, aunty," Ella said in a sweet, innocent voice as she received the unexpected gift.

"You're welcome, my child. Child of destiny," she proclaimed, admiring and hand-brushing her neat braids.

"Thank you for the sweet, ma. I sell clothes," Ella's mother replied.

The jovial Nigerian woman handed her a pass as they made their way toward the door.

The other travelers were already on Nigerian soil, waiting on Tabi. The girl, wearing the conspicuous lip gloss that for some reason seemed to bother Mr. Bara, who had sat by Chefor, stood in impatience—pacing restlessly and constantly checking her watch.

"Oga, well done-o."

"Thank you, sir," Tabi replied.

A male Nigerian officer leaned on the right front door with his arms and partially sent his head through the window into the car. "Oga, come and open the boot," he said casually as though it was something he didn't really care about but had to do for formality.

"OK, sir. No problem," Tabi replied as he opened the door and moved toward the trunk, where he was met by the officer.

The officer waited until he opened the trunk, and they were both obscured by it before he launched his maneuver. "Oga, settle. Why are you behaving as if you don't know?" he asked with an imposing smile that told Tabi he wasn't really joking.

Tabi took his wallet out of the back pocket of his faded jeans and handed a few naira notes to the officer. "Take, sir. That is your settlement."

"Correct! Now you're talking!" he said with a smile, hastily slotting the notes into his pocket. "Good! Safe journey." The officer ostentatiously touched a few bags and shut the trunk.

• • • • • • • • ● ○○○○○○○○○ ○ ○

Back in the Cameroon immigration building, Chefor burned with a desire to ask Mrs. Chakunte why she too could not speak English since

Cameroon was a country of both languages, but he knew better than to get on her nerves. There could be consequences—and there undoubtedly would be. "Northwest. I am from the Northwest Region." So, Chefor said instead. But she sat still, folding her arms and squinting her eyes with a penetrating scrutiny as if to invade his very mind. *But why? Why was an exercise meant to take only a moment suddenly turning into an interrogation? Others had taken just a few minutes,* Chefor worried.

Mrs. Chakunte looked at her phone again and then back to his face. Her phone, and back to his face—as though trying to match a resemblance. Then calmly but suspiciously, she said, "Which tribe are you from?"

"Santa," Chefor replied, wondering why his tribe was necessary. "I was born and bred in Santa."

"Yes, you'll be going back there," she said emphatically, widening her eyes as if to ensure that her statement was completely clear. Then she dialed a number. "Calling Monsieur Jean," the tiny electronic programmed voice said as the iPhone behind her rang from where it was charging. She sucked her teeth and madly dropped her phone on the table before swiftly exiting her office as though to launch an attack.

"What?" Chefor asked, increasingly pissed. "I have the right to travel any time I want." His eyes were turning red. He'd had just about enough of this frivolousness and wanted it to stop.

But it was only beginning.

"Terrorist," she mumbled.

Her urgency made Chefor tremble in fear as he beheld the gigantic woman. *What have I done? Why is she so furious with me? And the abrupt rush—what is the emergency?* A thousand whats and whys flooded his cerebrum, which provided not an answer to any.

The black Samsung Galaxy S9 on the table exuded a pale whitish light and repeatedly blinking images in a video.

For some reason, perhaps his intuition, Chefor decided to spy. And when he did, his eyes widened in disbelief as his heart sank in shock.

A Facebook video was playing on mute. In it, a monstrous crowd was marching with branches of African peace plants and placards through a greenish scenery he recognized as oddly familiar. Suddenly, a signboard appeared: Government Bilingual High School (GBHS), Santa.

A gorgeous albino guy in a colorful sweater dashed in front of it. His left hand held a long eucalyptus stick that hoisted a blue plastic bag, and his right was folded into a fist that he threw into the air as his lips moved as though chanting a song of victory. By him was a bulky, overzealous guy in a sky blue sweater, hands thrown in the air with a placard: "Yes to an Inclusive Dialogue, Yes to a Two-State Federation."

My world! Chefor's mouth hung open and could have captured a hundred flies had he been at his hometown's local slaughterhouse. "Who is that?" he mumbled, horror-struck, refusing to acknowledge it was him, but it was indeed. Enthusiastically jubilating next to the albino guy, in the protest that had rocked Anglophone Cameroon, of which he had been a passionate participant. That day, everyone had worn or held a blue or white item. Colors on a flag that represented both their struggle and their identity. "My world," he whispered, placing his hand over his chest. He felt his heart pound so hard it was a miracle it did not burst through his chest. "What will I do?" he asked, canvassing the empty room as though its old blank walls could give him an answer.

The sudden realization that Mrs. Chakunte had indeed been matching his resemblance, sent chills down his spine. And the fact that he wore the same sweatshirt from that day propelled him straight into pacing. Three steps to the left, three steps to the right. Left, right, up, down. "What will I do?" he asked again. Except this time, his voice was daunted, and he began punching his left palm with his right fist. Then left, right, up, and down he went.

Chefor was aware of what awaited him. The military had gunned down some of his friends that day and arrested others for lesser "crimes." Yet here he was, in a 3-D Samsung Galaxy video. Brandishing in capital letters, everything the dictatorial government stood against. *What are my options?* he thought. *Should I try* choco *(bribe)? Or should I take off like a Sahara cheetah?*

CHAPTER 2

TABI'S VEHICLE STOOD to the right of the immigration building, a few meters into Nigeria. Everyone stood by it, impatiently waiting on Chefor.

Ella no longer clung to her mother, and her eyes were no longer closed. In fact, they were wide-open as she stood by her mother, quietly sucking on the pink lollipop and staring at the twenty-six-year-old girl with the red lipstick, who began nagging loudly.

"What is happening? I really hate waiting!" she yelled. "Driver, get us out of this place. What is he still doing over there?"

"Calm down. I'm sure he'll be here any minute from now," a beautiful bronze-skinned lady said.

Not that it was his business, but Bara was dying to know why this girl wore lipstick on such an unstable and cold morning.

"Some say this is our new normal, but I could never get use to this," he said, as the gunshots across the border in Cameroon were becoming even louder.

"OK, I just have to ask. Why are you wearing lipstick?" He exhaled deeply. It was such a relief to finally get it off his chest.

"And why are you wearing oversized suit pants over a pair of tennis shoes?" she fired back after slowly inspecting him from head to toe and back to head. "And a green baseball cap over a black turtleneck sweater? What is wrong with you?" she added to the amusement of everyone.

"Shut up," Bara responded.

"You asked for it," Ella's mother said, amused as everyone else. "What's your name dear?"

"I'm Claudia," she replied.

Claudia was not an uncommon name, but she was so fun of it, and there was an exoticness to the way she called it, that charmed just about anyone.

"Well, I think you look fabulous. In this ruthless war that has seized our reality as we knew it, at least one of us should." Ella's mother said.

"Exactly! It has taken so much from me already and I won't let it keep taking. And thanks for the flattery, dear. Is this your daughter?"

"Oh, yes, she is."

"What's her name?" Claudia asked, reaching out for Ella's shoulder.

"Her name is Ella."

"Wow! Such a cutie."

"Yeah … a sassy one," Ella's mother replied, and they both laughed.

• • • • • • • • ● ○○○○○○○○ ○ ○

Chefor was still panting and pacing in dismay. And when he noticed that he still was wearing the sweatshirt, he took the damn thing off and hurriedly dumped it in the trash can by the door, just in case the woman was still in doubts of what she'd seen, but even he knew the odds were high.

He realized the first option was unlikely to guarantee him any success. They'd probably take the money and still have him locked up or killed anyway. So, he considered the later. To spring off like a cheetah, but in which direction would he run? He turned and saw Monsieur Jean and Mrs. Chakunte heading toward him from outside. Jean's face burned with a fury, and the pair of cuffs that dangled from his left hand explained everything.

Instantly, Chefor became overwhelmed by an avalanche of emotions that took over his saneness and his very ability to think. "God, help me," he said. He'd never had any issues with his legs, but they suddenly felt weaker. His entire body trembled and then froze. Even though he was paralyzed by fear, the thought of the repercussions awaiting him provoked an immediate flow of adrenaline. He felt everything more intensely and saw everything more clearly. So, in the spur of that moment, and like a true African cheetah, he dashed through the side door that served as a second entrance onto the bridge, directly from the immigration room.

"Look, he's escaping!" Mrs. Chakunte pointed at Chefor.

"Let's go!" Jean commanded as they turned around and made their way through the main gate.

Chefor was already on the bridge, fleeing as fast as his legs could carry him. He aimed toward the Nigerian border as Monsieur Jean and Mrs. Chakunte chased after him with unwavering determination.

A deafening gunshot from behind brought him to an unanticipated halt.

"Stop—or I will shoot!" Mrs. Chakunte yelled.

Chefor stopped but dared not turn around.

Monsieur Jean sprinted toward him with the handheld metallic detector in his pocket and the cuffs in his hand. Mrs. Chakunte followed closely behind with the short gun in her hand as though she were chasing an armed thug.

Chefor reluctantly raised his hands in surrender as they closed in on him. Then he noticed his black suitcase abandoned by the Nigerian immigration building and the red vehicle leaving. Tabi and his traveling companions had noticed that all wasn't well and were vanishing, leaving him behind to his fate. He quickly blinked back the tears that slowly gathered in his sad, round eyes, and then he folded his lips in defiance. He'd decided to put up a fight.

As Monsieur Jean attempted to cuff his hands behind his back, he launched an elbow straight to his eye. He had aimed for his tooth, but the eye was perfect.

"Bastard! He hit my eye. Son of a bitch!" Jean screamed. He reached out to feel the eye that was now bulging like a tropical fruit. Chefor turned and kicked the slender man between his legs with a strength meant to shatter the saggy pair of slimy spheres that carried his very essence.

"He has … he has …" Jean was unable to finish the sentence as a sharp pain pierced his stomach, causing him to coil like a heated rubber. He twisted his face and cupped his hands over his manhood in excruciating agony.

"I will shoot! I will shoot!" Mrs. Chakunte yelled.

The Nigerian immigration officers were filming—perhaps the reason why she had not shot yet.

Monsieur Jean used his leg and swept Chefor with the prowess of a seasoned karateka.

As Chefor staggered and tried to regain his stability, he knocked the gun out of Mrs. Chakunte's hand, sending it meters away.

Mrs. Chakunte punched his nose, which sent him straight to the ground, and then she descended on him with a storm of blows.

"Help! Help me!" Chefor screamed, but no one came to his rescue.

Monsieur Jean was gathering himself up, and Chefor knew he was about to be overcome.

Mrs. Chakunte sat on him, but Chefor blocked her blows with his left arm and quickly maneuvered his right around her neck. He pulled her closer and bit her chunky jaw with his fangs.

She cried out for mercy. "Help! Help!"

Chefor held on, sinking his incisors deep into her flesh blood began oozing out. "Help me, monsieur!" she cried again, trying to grab Chefor's neck.

Suddenly, a sequence of kicks landed steadily on Chefor's ribs. Jean was up and booting the life out of him. "Bastard, imbecile, son of a bitch," he cursed.

Chefor screamed in anguish, letting go of Mrs. Chakunte's jaw. His teeth were stained with blood and drops of it sprinkled on his white T-shirt.

Mrs. Chakunte quickly got up, and she was bleeding profoundly. A chunk of flesh hung from her jaw, leaving behind a scarlet cavity that would form an everlasting scar. "First aid! First aid!" Mrs. Chakunte held her jaw and ran toward the immigration building.

"Leave me alone! Let me be!" Chefor cried, completely drained.

"Shut your mouth!" Jean picked up the gun, grabbed Chefor's arms, and dragged him back to the immigration building.

• • • • • • • • ● ○○○○○○○○○ ○ ○

Chefor sat aghast in an empty room, his arms cuffed behind his back. He spat Mrs. Chakunte's blood out of his mouth as he cried. Sooner than later, he'd be transported to the regional prison in the army truck that stood at the rear end of the building. Its doors were dotted with bullet holes. Perhaps he'd be shot to death and dumped in a bush like they'd done with others.

He felt consoled that Monsieur Jean would not see with his right eye for a week or two—and Mrs. Chakunte would deal with a deformed face for the rest of her life. Even in death, he would remain an unpleasant memory. *The damn pompous woman discovered the video. It serves her right*, he thought.

CHAPTER 3

ENDLESS LINES OF automobiles filled the beautiful streets of Lagos. They blasted their horns in frustration of the stagnant traffic, and the grumbling sounds of electric generators filled the air as millions of Lagosians went about their business.

After three weeks in Nigeria, Claudia was dying to change her hairstyle. She stepped into a busy saloon in a pair of white sneakers, short denim overalls, and an immaculate white fitted T-shirt she had carefully folded the sleeves and said, "I'm Claudia." She stood purposely in the center of the room to attract attention.

"I'm Ngozi," one of the workers replied, clearly admiring Claudia's impeccable fashion.

"Do you braid?" Claudia asked.

"We do everything, Ma."

"Claudia. The name is Claudia," she said.

"Sorry, Ma," Ngozi said.

"Really?" Claudia asked.

"Claudia," Ngozi corrected herself, and they both smiled. "Please have a seat." She pointed to the shiny blue stool that faced the voluminous mirror, which was pinned to the wall over a table that was filled with gels, combs, and hair products.

Chima sat under an air dryer, constantly blushing as she browsed on her phone.

Yep, someone is definitely asking her out, Claudia decided. Then she side-eyed another costumer who sat about five feet away from her, having his hair lugged by three women in blue aprons. *That's breathtaking,* she thought.

"You know what, Ngozi? I've changed my mind. Let's do lugs instead," she said eagerly.

"OK, dear. As you wish, but the price will be different." Ngozi began sectioning her gorgeous, thick, ebony afro.

"I can pay. Go on," Claudia said. Bored by the sudden awkward serenity in the saloon, Claudia extended a hand to pick up a magazine from the table. She dangled her fingers as if to show her nails, which were polished in red to match the red bandana that she'd tied her afro and her ever-present red lipstick. The headline on the magazine's front page almost crushed her: "The Buhari's Government Unlawfully Extradites Southern Cameroons Leaders." She said, "What?"

Ngozi shuddered, and everyone paused and dazed at their direction.

"What's wrong, madam ... Claudia?"

"Our leaders have been extradited. My god, this is horrible news. I don't think it'll be safe for me to remain in Nigeria. I could be sent back to Cameroon. To my death." Claudia responded.

"Eya! I heard the situation in Cameroon is getting worse daily," said Nketchi, the shortest of them all, in Nigerian pidgin English.

"I'm sorry dear," Ngozi said as they all resumed work. "I did not know you were from Cameroon." She pronounced it "Kemeroon."

"I am," Claudia responded regrettably, almost wishing she weren't.

"Eya!" Nketchi said again.

"But there isn't any extradition agreement between Cameroon and Nigeria," said the customer under the dryer.

"What's that?" Nketchi asked.

"It's a big book, my sister," another woman responded.

"Then how do you expect me to know? Did I go to school? Anyway, that is how our African leaders behave, my dear. They do not care about the law. Eya! Sorry, OK. It is well," Nketchi assured.

The guy with the lugs said, "There are still thousands of Cameroonian refugees in Nigeria, but considering this, their stay here seem unpredictable. I think you should run. Run away to somewhere far. Out of the continent I suggest. If Nigeria can send you back, they'll make every other African country do the same. There's a reason they're called the giant of the continent."

Everyone nodded in agreement.

"Thank you," Claudia said dryly as she thought of her options for a safe heaven.

CHAPTER 4

THE CITY WAS plastered with lights as the flying bird succumbed to the annoying pull of gravity. It decelerated to a halt and gracefully opened its doors. The passengers exited in a line, mostly carrying backpacks. In the busy airport, hundreds of people seemed to be in a rush.

At each of the checkpoints, immigration officers processed the travelers. In the luggage claim area, suitcases of different colors and sizes were traversing the scanners on a baggage carousel.

"Welcome to Ecuador!" The immigration officer at checkpoint 3 stamped the passport of a guy who claimed to be a tourist from Bahrain.

Bara stood by him at checkpoint 4, holding his file of documents. "Where are you from, sir?"

"From Cameroon, madam," he replied. He didn't like the sinister tone that lingered in her politeness, but he shook it off and decided to answer every question boldly.

"What is your name—and what are you here for?" She smiled as she flipped the pages of his passport.

Why would she ask that? The name is right there in the passport, Bara thought. "My name is Bara Johnson, and I'm here visiting."

"Here visiting?" she repeated, passionately stressing every word. "Can I see your documents?"

"Oh, yes, of course," Bara replied with confidence.

"For how long do you intend to stay?" she asked.

"A month, madam. Thirty days." Bara smiled and handed her the stack of papers he'd taken out of his file.

"How much cash do you have on you, sir?"

"A thousand and five hundred dollars," Bara replied.

"How convenient. Security! Take him away," she called, still smiling.

"What? What have I done?" Bara asked, surprised and angry.

"Sorry, sir, you have to wait in there." A stern-looking officer pointed to a door at end of the checkpoints.

"But why should I?" Bara demanded.

"Just wait in the damn room!" The guard snatched Bara by the arm and pulled him toward the room.

The drowsy officer behind the counter said, "Can you please place your right thumb on the blue surface before you, sir? The rest of your fingers please. Can you please repeat the process with your left fingers? Can you please repeat the name of your country for me?"

"Cameroon," Bara replied.

"Your name, sir. Can you please repeat your name for me?"

"Bara Johnson, but may I know why I'm—"

"I'm done. You can take him away," the officer said.

"Answer me! I have a right to know why my information is being collected!"

The guard dragged him down the narrow corridor and pushed him to the floor of a small room.

"Let me out of here! Let me out!" He ran toward the heavy metal door that was slowly shutting before him. "I will call the human rights department!"

The stonehearted guard disappeared, wholly unmoved.

"Release me!" He banged on the door with both hands, but it was firmly closed, trapping him within.

Bara bounded his face against the thick metal door and shut his eyes. He felt like he was trapped in a spider web. *Nope, those flies eventually get eaten, for God's sake.* He took a deep breath, and as he released it, he heard voices speaking in Spanish.

His file had fallen when the guard pushed him to the floor. As he turned to pick it up, he noticed another guard sitting on the couch. He was watching a TV program about women struggling to lose weight.

"Girls to the left, boys to the right, living room for all," the guard said.

"I'm sorry, what?" Bara asked.

With his eyes glued to the TV, the guard repeated, "Girls to the left, boys to the right, living room for all." It sounded like a verse he'd memorized and recited a million times.

Bara scanned the room. A few feet from the door, three couches were in a semicircle, and a fifty-inch TV was suspended on the wall. Behind the couches, was a little space between two doors that faced each other. The English translation beneath the Spanish labels said "male" on one and "female" on the other. There was no sign for a bathroom anywhere. Perhaps they were connected to each of the rooms from the inside.

"Whatever," Bara mumbled after chewing his teeth. Completely defeated, he picked up his file and slumped down on the floor.

CHAPTER 5

IN A SECLUDED part of the city, a police officer pulled four young Indian men out of a taxi.

"Please, sir. Please, sir. *Por favor,* sir. Our documents are still in process at immigration."

"Where are you off to?" he asked in a google-translated text on his phone.

"We're on our way back to our hotel, sir. We went for dinner in town," a tall Indian guy replied in his own google-translated text.

"But you should not be out at this time without proper documentation," the officer wrote.

"It's just ten at night, sir, and we each have the temporary receipts given from immigration while our residences are being processed."

"No, it's too late to be out with those receipts. They are soon to expire."

The Indian guy twisted his face.

"One line! What's your name?" the officer demanded.

"Sajid, sir. My name is Sajid Pal." He shoved his phone back into his pocket.

"Everybody, behind him!" The officer pointed at Sajid.

They reluctantly lined up behind him and grumbled in Punjabi.

The crafty bald officer began searching them and pulling out every dollar he found.

"But our receipts have not expired, sir," cried the third in line whose one hundred dollars had just been snatched.

"Me ... take you ... police ... deportation ... back India," the officer said. "Go!" He yanked a twenty out of the last guy's back pocket, dashed to his vehicle, and vanished.

Their taxi driver began blasting his horn. They drove off in the taxi, knowing he'd only exploited them because they were foreigners—and there was absolutely nothing they could do about it. That hurt.

•••••••••●○○○○○○○○○ ○

Back at the airport, Bara and the guard were ignoring each other.

There's just a lot of foolishness everywhere, Bara thought as he sat on the couch with his poor file on his lap. *What made the woman want to know how much money I had? And why wasn't it a factor for everyone else, especially the Middle Eastern guy at the adjacent counter? He seemed to have had a question-free reception. What was so different about me? Was it my race? Or where I'd come from? And that woman I thought was an ageless beauty when I approached the counter, she's ugly.* He now decided. *And what was with the smiles? Cunning bitch. I knew there was something behind those smiles. Immigration officers are not known to be nice. Foolish me, I ignored it and smiled along like a stark buffoon.*

One of the women in the TV show fell off the treadmill, and her belly fat wobbled.

The officer smiled.

Someone in the men's sleeping room snored and then farted loudly.

Bara sent a guilty side glance to the officer, but he pretended not to notice.

The TV played a beer commercial. In it, a tall, slender white guy in a black suit was flirting with a bunch of hot supermodels in an overcrowded bar. *Lucky bastard,* Bara thought. His mouth watered. *God! I would kill for a beer.*

His thoughts strayed to a vacation he had taken at the beach in his country. His eyes closed, his face brightened with a wishful smile, and his mind dissolved in memories of the women, the countless choices of beer, the fine sand, the cold Atlantic Ocean breeze massaging his face, and then the music stopped. His eyes opened, and his smile faded. The commercial was over. The officer coughed and seemed just as miserable as Bara was.

Of course, he'll get a check at the end of the month. But he seems like a paid prisoner. The guy could have been home with family or at a job where he'd be allowed to use his phone. He must have never thought of guarding a school, a hospital, a bank, or somewhere else. Here, he's locked up like a criminal, with hopeless immigrants, and watching a weight loss show. Really! A weight loss show? He shook his head. *Well, I guess someone has to do the job.*

"Bara?" a voice called from behind. It sounded familiar. "Jesus, Bara! What are you doing here?" Kingsley asked in Nso, their native tongue.

"Oh my God!" Bara did not believe his eyes. It was Kingsley. His cousin had been sleeping in the room the whole time. "What? Kid bro!" Bara dropped his file on the floor. "Kingsley, what are you doing here?"

"Bara, what are *you* doing here?" Kingsley switched to English.

They embraced and answered questions with questions like typical Africans.

Kingsley was fighting back tears "I've been here for five days."

"Five days?" Bara said.

"Yes. They said they were sure I'd lied about my age. They wanted to verify if I was truly twenty-one."

"Flimsy," Bara muttered. "So, it's been you farting in the room the whole time?" Bara smiled.

"No, that would be Hassan. He's from Sierra Leone. He is lactose intolerant," Kingsley said.

The door rattled and opened for an immigration officer. His name tag said Gonzales. The guard quickly got up from the couch as if he'd been expecting him. The two men mumbled to each other, and Gonzalez advanced toward them with his hands in his pockets.

Kingsley crossed his fingers and said a prayer.

"Three hundred dollars each—or you'll be sent back to your country," Gonzales said.

"We are ready," Kingsley said before Bara could object. "We are ready, sir."

Bara nodded.

"Leave the money in the bathroom and have yourselves ready to go." The guard glanced at the cameras on the roof.

Hassan detonated another fart.

"Wake him up! I expect to receive nine hundred dollars in total." Gonzales turned and spoke in Spanish to the guard.

CHAPTER 6

DOWNLOAD FAILED—TRY AGAIN. No connection. Download failed—try again. Sajid was standing in front of his hotel room. For hours, he had been trying to download pictures of his newborn daughter. Seeing her was going to help him forget the unfortunate incident that night, but the hotel's Wi-Fi had expired, and the phone signals were spotty.

"Hello … it's me … I've been wondering if aft—"

His phone began playing Adele's "Hello." Great! It was his girlfriend. He answered it at the first ring. "Hello! Do you hear me? Hello! Mira, do you hear me? Fuck!" He almost threw his phone off the balcony. *Nope*! It was an iPhone X for crying out loud. He raised it and stepped to the left. Then to the right. To the right and back to the left. A bar of cell service appeared. Then a second and a third. The third disappeared—and so did the first two. "Shit!"

• • • • • • • • ● ○○○○○○○○○○ ○

Bara stood with Hassan and Kingsley in front of the Quito International Airport, quivering in the biting cold. "Jesus! It has got to be freezing in hell." Hassan was shaking like a leaf in the harmattan.

"I thought you were a practicing Muslim," Kingsley said.

"I'm a practicing everything, boy—even Jew," Hassan responded.

"I bet you are," Bara said with a laugh.

Kingsley seemed startled by a Muslim mentioning the name of Jesus.

A taxi pulled up in front of them.

"Let me." Hassan tilted his head down to the window and spoke in fluent Spanish. "Hello! Can you take us to this hotel?" He held out his phone.

"OK, my friend. Let's go," the driver said.

"Wait, my friend. How much are you charging?" Hassan asked.

"He speaks Spanish?" Bara was amazed as Hassan started bargaining with the driver.

"You have no idea. He speaks French too." Kingsley picked up his suitcase.

Hassan announced that the fare was seven dollars.

They put their suitcases in the trunk of the fancy yellow taxi and hopped in with their backpacks.

"Seven dollars? That's cheaper than I expected." Kingsley adjusted himself between the two other men.

"He priced it at ten dollars, but he did not resist when I offered seven," Hassan said.

"Where are you from, my friends?" the driver asked as he turned up the volume of the radio.

The beat was so infectious that Hassan couldn't resist swaying to it.

"Africa. We are from Africa," Hassan replied.

The driver nodded.

"Wow! Bro, I know I've said this before, but I really wish I was just as linguistic as you are. You'll have to give your guy some lessons," Kingsley said.

"How much will you be paying for an hour?" Hassan asked with a smile.

"Come on! OK, I'll pay you a million thank yous," Kingsley replied.

They all laughed.

They continued chitchatting.

The muscular driver was speeding faster as they approached a more secluded part of the city.

Bara noticed that the driver had deviated from the directions of the GPS on the phone he'd hung by the radio. "Ask him why he's not following the GPS directions? Why is he taking us somewhere else?"

"And tell him to turn down the volume," Kingsley added.

A sudden sense of paranoia crept in, and before Hassan could utter a word, the driver pulled over and parked on the side of the road.

"What is the problem, amigo?"

"What are you doing?"

"What's wrong?'

The driver pulled out a pistol and pointed it at Kingsley's head. "Give me your *telefono*. Give me your *telefono* or me shoot."

They raise their hands in surrender. Screaming would be futile.

The driver turned the radio to a deafening volume, and the closest building was fifty meters away. He moved the gun to Hassan each time he spoke to compel him to translate.

Kingsley rolled his eyes as the deadly metallic object pressed on his forehead. It sent chills down his spine. His body streamed hot sweat in the freezing cold. His heart pounded, and he could swear he felt it drop to his stomach. "My pocket ... my telefono."

"What is he saying?" the driver yelled, moving the gun to Hassan.

Kingsley released a deep breath of relief.

Hassan closed his eyes. "His ... his ..."

"Please—" Bara started.

"Shut up," the driver shouted and shifted the gun to Bara's face.

Bara shushed and pointed to the phone in the chest pocket of Kingsley's jacket.

The driver extended his left hand, pulled out Kingsley's iPhone, and pointed the gun at Hassan and Bara. They removed their old Samsung galaxies, but he did not want them. "Money! Give me money!"

"He's asking for money," Hassan said.

They pulled dollars out of their pockets and held them in their shaky hands.

"All," he yelled.

"That's all we have ... please." Hassan burst into tears.

"Out! Get out!" The driver grabbed the money from their hands.

They stumbled out of the vehicle with their backpacks and watched as he vanished with their suitcases.

Hasan sat on the sidewalk, completely defeated, and Bara sprinted off behind the disappearing vehicle.

They saw a hotel about fifty meters away. It wasn't the one they had set out for, but they didn't care.

Sajid said, "Madam ... Wi-Fi ... not work. Tomorrow ... me ... my friends ... go away."

"Calm, my friend. Tomorrow ... I tell you ... fix," the stunning receptionist said.

The hotel's bell rang, demanding her attention.

"Good evening, miss. My friends and I need a room please." Hassan passed their passports through the gate.

"Good evening." She collected the passports and looked suspiciously at the lost men.

Thank God they'd managed to escape with their backpacks and had been smart enough to not give the robber all their money. He'd been in such a hurry that he didn't have time to search them thoroughly.

"Welcome." She opened the gate. "We only have rooms for two or three persons."

"We need a room for three people. How much will that cost?" Hassan asked, searching his backpack for money.

"Ten dollars for a night, sir," she replied.

"Good. No problem. Guys, the room costs ten dollars a night." Hassan placed the money on the desk.

"Thanks, Hassan. We'll refund you later," Bara said.

"Room number 8." The receptionist handed Hassan the keys.

"That's right by our room. Come, my friends, I'll take you," Sajid said. "You look like hell, my friend. Are you OK, my friend?" He placed a hand on Kingsley's shoulder as they ascended the stairs.

"We just got robbed after spending three nights in jail. So, no, my friend. I am not OK," Kingsley replied. "I need to sleep on a real bed, and I need Hassan to eat something—anything—that for one night will not make him fart out his butthole and keep me awake with his constant bathroom trips."

"What?" Hassan smiled.

"You lost me," Sajid said.

"Never mind. I'm just tired. It's been a trying night."

"Oh yeah!" Sajid said. "Ecuador is breathtaking, but it can also be quite trying. My friends and I are actually leaving in two days."

"Good for you, bro." Bara said. "All I need right now is to dump myself in bed. Where do you get food around here? I'll be needing about four plates of rice when I wake up."

Hassan opened the room, which had a balcony that was six feet wide and twenty feet long.

· · · · · · · · ● ○○○○○○○○○ ○

At the Ecuador-Colombia border, a checkpoint building linked both countries. Colombian police officers roamed about, and a few vehicles were in front of the building. Two were carrying the Indians and Bara with his friends. The foreigners were ordered into the tiny building, and their chauffeurs were told to not wait.

The Ecuadorians asked them who they were, where they came from, and why they'd come. The Colombians had no time for chitchat. They knew exactly what they wanted and went straight for it.

"One line! And take off your shoes," one of the officers ordered.

They took off their shoes and stood in a line as the officers began searching their shoes, backpacks, and pockets. From each person, they would take a twenty- or ten-dollar note. The immigrants had learned not to trust anyone—not even the police. Before leaving the hotel, they had hidden their money in the most obscure places. Leaving some bills in their pockets was a trick to conceal the rest of their money.

"Spanish! Anybody?" asked an officer behind a table at the rear of the room.

"We're each going to move to the table and write down our names, ages, countries and also give our fingerprints," Hassan translated after the officer.

After providing each of them with a five-day permit to stay in Colombia, the officers transported the migrants to Cali. They said it was the best they could do.

Cali was warm and vibrant. The booming roadside music, the food, the jovial people, and the countless bars were all very tempting, but the group did not stay. Couldn't afford to. Five days was not a lot of time, and they could not risk exceeding it because they'd be returned to Ecuador. So, they boarded a night bus to Medellin. Hassan said it offered more. From diversity to acceptance.

In a few hours, they were speeding on the meandering road, ascending and descending the never-ending hills that were both petrifying and enthralling at the same time.

It seemed to be countless hours in the bus before they finally arrived the bus terminal that Kingsley swore was ten times bigger than the airport back home in Cameroon. "My goodness! Bara!" he said.

"I know, bro! I know," Bara replied.

From Hassan's earlier account, Medellin was verifiably beautiful. Especially with the night ambiance, it was stunning to say the least.

They exited the crowded station with their backpacks and hired two cabs to the nearest and most affordable hotel they had found on Google

Maps. They approached the reception, and Bara, who was trailing the group thought he heard a voice that rang a bell. Then he heard a statement that completely cleared his doubts and shocked him to the core.

"I'm Claudia."

"What!" Bara said, pushing his way forward through the group. He pushed one of the Indians so hard you would have thought they had a problem. "Claudia!" he called with intense excitement plastered all over his face. "What are you doing here?

"Bara! My God! Bara, what are you doing here?" Of course she answered with a question. She was an African after all.

"It's a very long story," Bara answered as they caught each other in a tight hug. One would have thought they were longtime lovers. They hugged so tightly and passionately that everyone expected a kiss.

"Hello!" Claudia waved to the others as she and Bara finally released each other. They answered in a chorus, and Kingsley caught one of the Indian guys winking.

Claudia wore ripped jeans and a sweatshirt. She looked quite exhausted, but even that did not take a thing away from her glaring beauty. "I was trying to get a room. It's been an awfully long journey, and I'm really glad to meet someone familiar."

"Yeah! Tell me about it. We've had a horrible experience ourselves," Bara said tiredly.

"How about we secure the rooms first," Hassan suggested, moving toward the receptionist.

· · · · · · · · · ● ○○○○○○○○○ ○ ○

With beautifully made soft beds, spotless bathrooms, air conditioning, and immaculate walls suspending Samsung flat-screen televisions, the rooms were the best they'd seen in a long while. Except for Claudia, they'd all chosen rooms with multiple beds.

Sajid sat on the spotless white toilet. A part of him wondered why, like him, many people found comfort reading or browsing in the bathroom, particularly while sitting on the toilet. Then he went on a video call with his baby mama. He was laughing and chatting in Punjabi while his friends were already, perhaps, on their third or fourth dreams.

In the next room, Kingsley jumped out of bed and rushed to the bathroom. On his way out, he heard moaning and groaning in voices he thought he recognized. "Damn you, bro," he muttered as Hassan snored and thundered as usual. The obscene but tempting groans continued for a while before he noticed that Bara was not in his bed. "Son of a bitch," Kingsley whispered with a smile. Bara had sneaked out and was getting down with Claudia in the next room. "I don't blame you, bro. I don't blame you at all," Kingsley said as he slipped beneath his blanket, aware that sleeping from then on might be nearly impossible.

The noises finally hushed, and Kingsley went back to sleep.

It seemed like minutes, but hours had passed, and Hassan was already up and about, visiting from one room to the next. "Let's go get some food please! I'm about to eat someone," he declared as he pulled the blanket away from Kingsley.

"What? Put that back. I'm trying to regain the time I missed yesterday to Bara and Claudia."

"The time you missed to ... no way!" Hassan was only now realizing that Bara was not in bed when he woke up, and he was not on the balcony or in Sajid's room.

"Yeah, way!" Kingsley replied.

"Honestly, I'm not entirely surprised," Hassan said as he threw the blanket back on Kingsley. "After that hug yesterday, it was to be expected. Wake up, man! Let's get some food. I'm dying." He slumped on his bed to keep him awake.

"Oh my God, Hassan! Why did I ever know you?"

"To bring light into your life, boy," Hassan joked.

"Shut up," Kingsley replied with a grin as he rose drowsily and staggered into the bathroom.

"Walk of shame!" Hassan said when Bara came into the room and picked up his backpack from the little table by his bed.

"What are you talking about, Hassan?" Bara asked pretentiously, trying to play dumb.

Kingsley stormed out of the bathroom with a toothbrush in his mouth and toothpaste foaming out of it. "How was it?"

"How was what? Go spit out that toothpaste. I can hardly hear a word you're saying." Bara tried to suppress a smile.

"Exactly! There, the smile of shame!" Hassan said.

"I'm not smiling, Hassan. Let's go eat something please. I'm starving," he said with a guilty smirk.

"Of course, you're starving. You got drained of all nutrients last night," Kingsley said as he stepped out of the bathroom.

"Obviously," Hassan said with a laugh.

"Guys, can we let this go? Nothing happened, OK?" Bara pocketed a few notes, picked up his phone, and started for the door.

"Yep! Let's just pretend that the sex noises I heard last night were in my dream," Hassan said, still smiling.

"Perhaps they were because, like I said, nothing happened."

"Yeah … says the guy who made it happen," Kingsley replied.

They all burst into laughter and headed out.

· · · · · · · · ● ○○○○○○○○○ ○ ○

Sajid and his three friends had no problem sharing beds. They'd taken a room with two beds and chatted and flipped through the TV channels.

"We need to go out tonight," Ram said as he leaped out of bed. "I'm tired of feeling miserable. If we've got just a few days to be here, I might as well shake to some Colombian rhythm."

"I agree. That's a fantastic idea," Aadesh said.

"Of course, you do, you just wanna be with a girl," Sajid replied.

Jonte said, "I don't think I've ever heard Colombian music before. I'll be lost on the dance floor."

Ram said, "All you have to do is move your feet, bro. Close your hands. Take two quick steps to the right, then to the left, while slightly rotating your hands."

"OK, let me give it a try. Hands close, two steps to the right, two steps to the left," Jonte said as he attempted the dance. "How was that?"

"How about you find a girl, get some drinks, and just chill with her at the table?" Ram replied.

"Yeah, we're not letting anyone see that. Let alone a Colombian. That was horrible!" Sajid said as everyone laughed. "I'm not sure, guys. I might have to stay in."

"Sajid, please don't be a bore," Aadesh said. "We've had enough boredom already, bro. Besides, you're our translator."

"Oh! I know what it is. Just like Jonte, he cannot dance," Ram said.

"Yeah, he can't," Jonte said. "He'll definitely sit with me at that table."

• • • • • • • • ● ○○○○○○○○○ ○ ○

Bara and Kingsley sat in the roadside restaurant, talking about how nice it was that there were so many black people in Medellin.

"Do you think anyone could tell the difference between us and the black people here?" Kingsley asked.

"If we don't talk, I doubt anyone could," Bara replied.

"I just received a call from Sajid. Said they were planning on going out tonight and wanted to know if we'd be interested," Hassan announced as he came in with a plastic bag of fruit.

"It's quite scary, but I'm tempted to say yes. I mean, look at all these pretty damsels," Kingsley said as he inspected the waitress.

"Dirty boy," Hassan muttered, giving him a gentle nudge.

"Don't blame me. The eyes just do what they do. Can't help it, bro," Kingsley said.

"Why is it scary?" Bara asked as they began eating.

"Bara, this place might be lively and beautiful—but don't forget who you are. A migrant with a five-day ultimatum to get out of this country. Five days out of which we've spent two. We have to keep that in mind, bro."

"I guess so," Bara said.

"I'm sorry. The soup is too spicy. I can't finish it." Kingsley pushed his bowl aside.

"I advised you to stick with what you know. Drink some water," Hassan said.

"Yeah, I'll just order some rice and take it home with me since you're almost done eating."

"Hola!" Kingsley said to the waitress he'd developed an instant crush on. Her response made him blush, but the moment was quickly ruined by his terrible attempt at Spanish, which provoked both pity and laughter.

Hassan said, "He needs a plate of rice and chicken to take home please. And he also thinks you're beautiful."

"Thank you," the girl responded cheerfully. Minutes later, she was giggling with her colleague at the counter.

"Yes! I think she's writing down her number for me. Stop looking!" Kingsley whispered. "It'll make her uncomfortable."

The girl picked up a piece of paper and the plastic bag that contained Kingsley's rice and started for their table.

"She's coming!" Kingsley was unable to compose the countless emotions tumbling within him.

"Hola. Thank you." The girl smiled, placed the plastic bag and the piece of paper before Kingsley, and walked to another table.

"Take the number, Hassan. You know I don't have a phone," he said as he swiftly picked up the paper.

"Lucky boy! It's not your fault you're too fine," Bara said.

"I'm all ears. Give the number—and let's go please. I'm all ears," Hassan said.

The smile that graced Kingsley's face slowly faded.

"What's wrong? Give me the numb—"

"Shut up, Hassan. It's the stupid bill," Kingsley replied.

"What?" Bara choked out the water in his mouth, and it splashed on the table. "Sorry. I'm sorry."

"Shut up, Bara. Have some compassion," Hassan said as he tried to control his own laughter. "I'm sorry, bro. You're still the finest guy. Let her go to hell."

Bara was literally in tears. He was laughing endlessly and attracting the attention of the other customers. "Sorry. I'm so sorry," he kept saying.

Kingsley rose and placed the payment on the disappointing piece of paper while refusing to tip the girl.

As they proceeded out, Bara did not stop laughing.

• • • • • • • • ● ○○○○○○○ ○ ○ ○

"Strawberries! Anything with strawberries." Claudia was greatly relieved to learn the waiter could speak English.

"How would you like it, miss?"

"Claudia. Call me Claudia. And I'll have it cold please," she said.

With Kingsley's words in mind, Bara had cautioned that they shouldn't go far into the city. So, that evening, they settled comfortably in a place about a mile away from their hotel.

There were tables for two and four with boys and girls being carelessly intimate and countless choices of wine visible behind the busy black bartender.

Bara insisted the bartender looked exactly like his classmate back home. The lights were dimmed for the couples on the dance floor, and they kept touching each other. It was simple but jolly, full of regular people who just wanted to have fun.

The two groups of migrants sat a table next to each other. All eyes were on them. A lot of the locals were either fascinated or perplexed by their style. The colorful turbans over a casual Western look was indeed alien, but it would have been a lie to say that it did not suit them.

Hassan appeared absent. Hassan was usually like that. His personality fluctuated too much to be normal—a constant swing from cheerful to depression, funky to moody, even when the situation or scenario did not warrant it.

Kingsley thought, *well, who really knows what anyone is going through?*

Claudia leaned over and grabbed Bara's arm.

Kingsley asked, "Are you guys, like, dating now?"

"Not at all! We are just friends," Claudia answered rashly as she quickly released Bara's arm and took a sip of the strawberry juice that only added the red to her lipstick.

The DJ kept playing traditional salsa music.

Jonte tried to move to the rhythm, but it was harder than Ram had described.

Ram said, "I'm going to dance. And you, my friend, should find that girl and just sit here with her like we agreed." He decided that two bottles of alcohol were enough for him.

"Shut up, Ram," Jonte replied playfully.

Ram was a surprisingly good salsa dancer—at least for a foreigner with no experience. It was not long before girls were taking their turns with him on the dance floor.

"I love Colombian girls!" Sajid proclaimed.

"You have a baby mama at home with a daughter," Aadesh reminded him.

"Let me live, Aadesh! Let me live!" Sajid started for the dance floor and was joined by everyone immediately. He was receiving his own fair share of girls—even though he was horrible at salsa. Even Hassan was up and killing the beat.

The Indians were puzzled at how easily and effectively the African guys danced to what they supposed was foreign music to them. Truth is, no music is fully foreign to an African. Perhaps Africa is really the origin of rhythm.

"Go, bro!" Kingsley cheered.

Fun Hassan was back again. Everyone joined in the merriment, and for a moment, they seemed to forget who they were, where they were, and how long they had to be there.

CHAPTER 7

THE MORNING WAS chilly but fresh, and Bara insisted on sitting in the tiny balcony. The breeze helped clear his hangover. Moments later, he was joined by Hassan, who seemed to be just as despondent as he was. "So, what now? Where do we go from here, bro?" Bara asked.

"Panama is our only option," Hassan replied as he moved to the edge of the balcony.

"Then what? What happens next? How do we even get there? What will become of us when our money is all finished? I left my country to resettle in Nigeria, bro. My Nigerian classmate from back in high school took me in."

"He went to high school in Cameroon?" Hassan asked.

"Yeah, we have outstanding high schools. Although it was partly because he is half Cameroonian. He moved to Lagos for university after graduation, but we remained in contact. We were close friends. I called him when the situation in Cameroon became unbearable, and he asked me to come right away. I was either going to use my bachelor's degree to find a job in Lagos or start a business with the money I'd saved from my previous business."

"So, why didn't you stay there?" Hassan asked.

"Nothing worked as planned," Bara responded.

"Ha! Does anything ever?" Hassan said.

"It seemed perfect for the first several weeks," Bara said.

"It always does," Hassan replied with a broken smile.

Bara said, "Then it all changed suddenly. People from my country were being extradited. Man, if I told you I was scared, it would be an understatement. I was terrified. My incredibly beautiful country is not a place to be in anymore. I yielded to his advice and came to Ecuador. I was going to learn Spanish and make a living from translating and teaching

English. That was the plan. That was the plan, bro. Not this. I did not plan for this at all. Now here I am—here we are—without as much as a plan for anything."

"You know, I was watching the news this morning," Hassan said.

"You were?"

"Yep! While you were giggling and chuckling with Claudia in the next room," Hassan answered with a smile.

"Shut up," Bara said playfully while giving him a slight push.

"You might as well just move into her room, bro. She seems to be your new addiction."

"She won't let me. She says we're just FWBs, and moving into her room will make things more serious than she can handle right now. Mind you, I don't even know what FWBs means. I figured it was probably a new slang, but I did not want to ask her. I didn't want her to think of me as old and boring."

"What?" Hassan was unable to stop laughing. "It's friends with benefits, bro. That's what it means. Oh my God! Man, you are so funny."

"Based on how you say it, I don't know if I should take it as a compliment or not."

They both laughed.

Bara said, "She made me realize how horrible I am at social colloquialism."

Hassan was in tears and laughing inexhaustibly at Bara. "No! Bara, you are funny. Kingsley must hear this story."

Bara said, "I should tell the story of how we met. It was at the border, standing in the biting cold, with that conspicuous red lipstick, complaining and yelling at everybody. It was hard to not take note of her. Our first words to each other were actually more like insults."

"That, my friend, is always the beginning of most true love stories," Hassan said.

Bara looked down at the road and noticed a police truck in the traffic. "Anyway, you were talking about the news."

"Yeah, that. You know what, bro? Let's talk about it later. Let's go buy our bus tickets for tonight and leave this place while we still can."

"I guess you're right, but where would we go?" Bara asked as they moved back in.

"The closest town to the border. We'll look on the map," Hassan replied.

"How about we all pack now since our room will expire in two hours? We can wait at the terminal until the bus leaves," Bara said.

"Yeah, that's brilliant. I'll let Sajid know," Hassan replied as they separated in the long empty corridor.

· · · · · · · ● ○○○○○○○○ ○ ○

Be it clothing, electronics, food, or games, there was something for everyone in the mesmerizing terminal that night. The migrants had talked the day away, and their bus was finally taking off.

"I'm going to miss this city," Kingsley said as he looked through the glass window.

"Yeah! Too bad we can't stay." Hassan leaned back as the bus slowly exited the terminal.

Medellin had been fun, and although the migrants had not been able to fully feel safe, it was the best time they had felt in a long while.

After a minute or two, the driver parked and dashed out of the vehicle. He came around, opened the passenger door, and demanded that the Africans exit the bus.

"What's going on, Hassan?" Bara asked as they stepped down.

"I have no idea. Guess we're about to find out," Hassan replied.

"I have a bad feeling about this," Claudia said.

"Yeah, so do I."

"Calm down," Kingsley said.

They stood by the bus, listening in wonder as Hassan and the driver went back and forth in what seemed to be an intense argument.

"What's going on Hassan? What is he saying?" Bara asked in frustration.

Hassan stood quiet for a moment to contain his anger and dismay. "He said we stink," he replied.

There was a silent degrading moment of shock and incredulity.

"Apparently there's a smell in the bus, and he and a few other passengers sitting in front with him believe we're responsible for it," Hassan explained.

"What?" Bara asked.

"My God! I have never been this humiliated," Claudia said with a hand over her chest.

"That's not even all. He's now threatening to leave us here. Claims the other passengers are not feeling comfortable," Hassan added.

"Wow!" Kingsley said.

"So, what happens now? He can't just leave us here. We already paid," Bara said as Sajid descended out of the bus.

"What?" he said. "Not good. Not good. This is not good, bro," he said, turning to the driver who was still in a heated altercation with Hassan. The driver seemed to be standing his ground, but luckily for the migrants, a few concerned locals came to their defense. They said they would get off the bus too and alert the police if he decided to kick out the foreigners.

They wanted to object to involving the police. Their past encounters with the uniformed men had, on the contrary, made their lives a living hell. They doubted this time would be any different, but the idea did seem to scare the driver. So, they let it and hoped to God it would not escalate to that point.

In the end, the driver yielded and allowed them in—on the disparaging condition that they move to the back seats. He returned with a bottle of perfume, and he shamelessly sprayed the immigrants and the section in which they sat.

"I can't believe that just happened," Claudia said as they drove off.

"I'm short of words myself," Kingsley said.

Claudia remembered the good times as she looked out at the glittering city lights. "You know what? I'm not going to let this man stain my mood or my perception of this beautiful city. The hate is with him, and it's on him to either deal with it or let it eat him up. I will not give him the power."

"Yep! He's definitely not worth it," Hassan said.

"Not one bit," Claudia said as they skimmed up and down the unbelievable hills in the opaque night.

· · · · · · · · ● ○○○○○○○○ ○ ○

A modest, open and outboard-powered panga boat harbored by the shore, constantly swaying as the ceaseless ocean currents flushed against it.

Bara and his friends checked out of the noisy transit station that stood about a hundred meters away from the shore. With their backpacks on their backs, they walked on the wooden walkway that was suspended by bars of wood and extended from the building toward the water. They'd been evaluated and given permits to transit through the waters.

Claudia stood at the edge of the four wooden stairs they eventually descended into the panga boat. In her opinion, it was really just a big canoe. She observed the transparent droplets that splashed as the waters hit the banks below her and retracted into lush blue waves that cascaded far across the endless waters. It was beautiful and awe-inspiring all at the same time.

Her imagination drifted to a documentary she'd seen about sharks. The horrifying fact that they were large enough to ingest an entire human being in a single gulp terrified her to the core. She wasn't exactly large! She was a bouncy, dainty girl a shark would gulp down in a second and probably think was an oversize fish. She shrugged at the thought, and then she took a step back and grabbed Bara by the arm.

"You're scared, aren't you?" Bara asked.

"Not really," Claudia lied.

"Me also. Not really," Bara lied too.

Truth was, they were all petrified. Ram was in tears.

"Is he going to be OK?" Hassan asked.

"No one is going to be OK, Hassan. Can't you see? Somebody, please wake me up from this dream!" Kingsley said.

"He has a phobia about large bodies of water," Sajid said as he gently patted Ram's back.

A man approached from the station behind them and distributed orange life jackets. Then he counted the thirty-five travelers and led them into the boat. A second boat was on its way to pick them up. All backpacks were collected and stored in the front of the boat.

"I don't think I can do this." Kingsley was shivering as they made their way into the swaying boat. They all sat together for moral support.

The panga boat had long wooden benches with no backrests. They had to hold on to the benches to keep themself from falling into the wild water. There was no coming back from such a fall, they were told.

The captain stood at the back, behind a thick glass that extended to his face and protected him from the breeze and any other distractions, and he ordered complete silence.

Throughout the journey, they were to avoid engaging in anything that could be a source of distraction to him. The outboard motor propelled the boat across the waters at a speed they neither expected nor believed.

The Pacific Ocean waters were not gentle at all. They were ravaging and wild. The deafening roar sent chills down their spines. They were not allowed to look back, but a few of them did, as the borders became fainter and fainter.

Ram sat between Sajid and Jonte. A stream of tears flowed down his cheeks. Sajid had told him not to, but he glanced at the mighty waves. Strange emotions rushed through his heart and set it pounding like a bass drum. His arms felt weak, and he could barely hold onto the bench beneath him.

Jonte thought, *Goodness, Ram is about to have a panic attack.*

Luckily, the boat seemed to slow down as it approached a checkpoint. A building with countless iron bars hosted dozens of policemen and policewomen. There were sighs of relief as they stopped for the inspection.

A tall, muscular police officer stepped out of the tiny room and ordered everyone to hold their permits in the air. Then, as if unsatisfied, he asked the captain to collect them and bring them up to him.

They passed their permits down to the captain.

The officer counted and matched the number of the permits to the migrants, and then he carefully examined each permit as he read out the names and redistributed them.

"Close your eyes," Hassan said loudly.

"What?" Ram asked.

Hassan said, "Sajid, tell him to close his eyes if he cannot handle the sight. The fear might go away or at least subside."

"Thank you, my friend," Ram said.

The exercise seemed brief, but it was effective enough. And before they could truly catch their breath, the boat was off and sailing again.

God! Where am I? Claudia thought. Claudia was from grassland Cameroon, so water was not her thing. There were no large water bodies in grass land Cameroon. Bara had been born there too, but he'd lived on the coast for half his life. Even though he'd gone to see the Atlantic a couple times, he'd never really been in the water. This was quite a different experience and certainly not the type he would have wanted.

They'd been riding for a little over an hour, and it felt like they'd entered a different section of the ocean. The waters were vicious and changed sharply from one color to another. Noisy, then silent. It became harder to tell which direction the waters went as they appeared to be spinning and flowing at the same time.

Hassan was no psychologist, but his advice made sense. Ram shut his eyes and decided he was going to open them for nothing but land.

Kingsley looked to his left and saw faint reflections of aluminum roofs piercing through the distant greenery. *That must be land,* he thought dreamily. The sight brought him no relief. They were riding parallel to it, and it was tens of miles away.

"Jesus! Jesus! Jesus!" they shouted across the boat.

A gigantic wave was steadily advancing toward them.

"Jesus!" Kingsley screamed.

The boat glided over the wave and was suspended in the air. Panga boats were not designed to cut through waves—they ride flat on them—but Kingsley did not know that.

They looked down, and a deep depression had formed on the surface beneath them. Trailing it was another wave, steady and unwavering.

This is the end, Kingsley thought.

They kept shouting to Jesus and other names in their languages and religions they believed could protect them.

Then, like a mighty stone, the boat landed heavily on the water. When it surged back up, it propelled and almost threw out its occupants. It effortlessly slid up and over the next wave, and it galloped for stability as it raced along.

Claudia struggled to keep her hold.

Bara thought, *If only I'd known, I would have tied her arm to mine. That way, I would have told her to relax and let go. Let me be her hero and hold on to the bench for us both.*

Kingsley looked back and across, but he saw nothing. The land was gone, and now he wished it was there. Far and indistinct, but there. All he could see now was water. Spanning miles and miles away. Vast and ravaging.

How fast is this thing going? Is it supposed to run this fast—or does this captain just not care? Kingsley thought as they raced past a smaller boat carrying three men. They were fishing, and it irritated him to the core. *If people must risk this much just to get fish, we all might as well become vegetarians. It's a better diet after all,* Kingsley decided.

Claudia found herself hating and complaining about everything. *In these waters, these life jackets are useless. They won't save us if anything goes wrong. They are completely useless. And orange! Really? Who makes anything in orange colors? ... Great! Now I'm thinking about the Titanic. Why would my mind choose now of all times to remind me of the* Titanic? *Look at this boat. Open and wide. I wonder if the captain checked the weather. God, we'll be damned if it rained.*

Another monstrous wave was approaching quickly.

"Not again," Bara whispered as they braced for it.

Sajid kicked Ram's leg. He thought it would be better if his eyes were open to prepare his mind for the landing. Once again, the boat glided over the roaring wave and into the air. It was suspended several meters above the water. It dropped with a mighty force that would have shattered the boat had it not been for the ever-present force of upthrust.

There were desperate cries all over. The woman sitting behind Kingsley vomited. Half-digested rice splattered onto Kingsley's back, gracing it with a warmth that felt both comforting and strange, but Kingsley was too focused on his safety to say anything.

The captain maneuvered and regained stability on the water, but great harm had already been done.

Aadesh had hit his knee against the boat when it landed, and blood was pouring out. There wasn't any first aid. He wailed and struggled to remain stable. *Damn it! If only I wore longer jeans,* he thought.

Hassan had been quite unbothered by everything. He seemed to take it as it came. He was surrounded by nothing but water, but he was parched. His lips felt shriveled and dry. He licked them. They were salty. He hated it. The ocean splashed nonstop on their bodies as the boat galloped along.

After three hours, there was still no sight of land.

Finally, an island settlement appeared miles away.

Kingsley exhaled in relief. "That must be our destination," he declared.

To his disappointment, they sailed past it from miles away. Like many in the boat, he'd thought the nightmare was over, but there were a few more such settlements to pass—and many more gigantic waves to overcome.

Ram was still bleeding profusely. He was losing too much blood. He ached for gulps of fresh water, but no one was going to risk letting go of the bench in order to drink. Ram felt weaker every passing minute, barely holding on as the boat flew ceaselessly and unmindfully.

They approached another settlement that appeared a little larger than the previous one. And even though Kingsley felt slightly excited and hopeful, he pretended not to be. *He's just going to speed past it. We're probably going to die here. I might as well atone for my sins. I have many of those.*

His heart leaped with excitement and then sunk in fear when the boat decelerated toward the multitude of people, including policemen. They stared from their hotel balconies and the wooden bridge that extended from the ocean to the island.

They all clapped and cheered for the captain as the boat finally settled.

A rope was thrown to the police officer, and he tied it to the bridge.

"Emergency! Emergency!" Sajid yelled.

Hassan and Jonte struggled to carry Aadesh. He'd bled for so long, and he was a minute away from completely passing out. So, while everyone else was scrambling to pick up their bags, Aadesh was being rushed to the island's health center.

CHAPTER 8

FROM THE LUSH greenery, the relaxed Afro-Caribbean vibe, the fresh ocean breeze that swept across the island every now and again, and the alluring restaurants exuding the best of local aromas, the island had much to offer. Anyone who set foot on it wanted to stay.

They admired the island and exchanged smiles with the shop owners as they walked to the island's immigration building.

"Sorry, my friend," the woman who had sat behind Kingsley said in Spanish as she passed by with her friends.

"What did she say?" Kingsley asked.

"She said she was sorry, but I don't think she meant it because she went on laughing immediately after."

"What was she apologizing for?" Hassan asked.

"I have no idea," Kingsley answered.

"Are you sure you didn't ask for her number, and she turned you down like the girl back in Medellin?"

"Bara, can you please let it go?" Kingsley said as they all began laughing. "As a matter of fact, had you not been here to translate, Hassan, I'd have thought she wanted my number."

"Really, bro! Come on, she could be your elder sister," Hassan joked.

"Well, she's not," Kingsley replied. "Look, bro, it was a miracle we made it out of that ocean alive. I've never experienced anything like that. Now, I understand how fragile life is and how, in the blink of an eye, it can all just become history. I don't know about you guys, but from now on, I won't pass on any entertainment that comes my way."

"Well, let's only hope it does come your way. It seems to really avoid you," Claudia said, provoking laughter once again.

"Shut up, Claudia," Kingsley said.

"What? That is the reason you can't get any girls. Never tell a girl to shut up. It's the first step toward losing her," Claudia said. "You're right about the journey though. It truly was a scary experience."

"I didn't take it that you were afraid. You seemed to be handling it well," Hassan said.

"Yeah, at least better than Ram. Poor guy had to keep his eyes closed for most of the journey," Bara added, secretly hoping that she would agree with Hassan. It crushed his heart to think that she needed him, but he'd done absolutely nothing to take away her fear.

Claudia said, "Hassan, for the first time in my life, I didn't care about my lipstick. It might sound stupid to you, but to me, it is scary on a whole different level."

They stepped into the immigration building, which was just an empty hall with a table by the door. It had neat gender-separating bathrooms.

"Talking about Ram, where are they?" Bara asked.

Claudia replied, "They hurried here before us. They must have gone out to the hospital to see Aadesh."

"We should go check on him later," Hassan said.

Kingsley went to answer his name at the table. The officer called out name after name, inspected the passes that permitted them entrance into the island and gave out five-day permits.

"This place is truly outstanding," Claudia said.

They headed into the island to find accommodation. Hundreds, if not thousands, of people from different parts of the world were going about in groups with their backpacks. It was pleasantly surprising how cosmopolitan the little island was.

"Are they all tourists?" Kingsley asked.

"I'm sure they are. There appear to be more hotels than private residences," Bara replied. "Wow! The owners must be making a lot of money."

They arrived at the modest-sized hotel that Hassan insisted would have looked better if they had painted it white. It would have made a stunning contrast with the dark green cypresses that shrouded its surrounding.

Dozens of people stood in groups, laughing and chitchatting.

"I swear, I've heard about five different languages already," Kingsley said.

"Ha! How can you tell they were different languages?" Bara asked.

"I think one can always tell when a language is different, perhaps from the sound," Hassan responded.

"Aunty Claudia!" a sweet little voice called from behind. "Aunty Claudia!"

"My goodness! Who just called me aunty in this place?" Claudia turned around. "What! My God! Ella! What in the world are you doing here? Bara, you do remember her, right?"

"Yeah, of course! The child at the border. What is she doing here, all by herself?" Bara replied.

"Where's your mother, sweetheart?" Claudia stooped down to meet the little girl.

"She's in the room ... she's pooping in the toilet," Ella answered innocently.

"Oh my God! Kids!" Kingsley said as they laughed.

"Oh, so she went into the bathroom, and you sneaked out to play with other kids?" Claudia said with a smile. "Not good at all. There are so many people here. You might get lost. Come on and take us to her." Claudia grabbed the little girl's hand.

They ascended the stairs and met Ella's mother in the corridor of the second floor. The child was lucky to return with delightful company. Her mother had planned to trash the life out of her or "beat some sense into her thick skull."

"It's a lie! Who am I seeing? Claudia!"

They screamed in glee as they ran and caught each other in a tight hug.

"It's me in the flesh, my dear. Good to see you again," Claudia said.

Not that they were longtime friends. It was unexpected to meet an old acquaintance.

Claudia said, "Unbelievable. Sis, what are you doing in South America ... on an island?"

"My dear, I should be asking you that question. What are you doing here? Wait a minute. I remember you ... Bara."

"Hello, sis." Bara smiled and gave her a brief hug.

"Nice to see you again." Ella's mother released the hug and exchanged handshakes with Kingsley and Hassan.

"We found Ella outside," Claudia reported.

Ella's mother said, "Thank you for bringing her back. Get in, Ella!" She ordered in clear vexation. "I instructed her to stay put. Then I went into the bathroom for two minutes, and she was gone."

The group went to her room.

A wooden bunk bed stood at the extreme left. At its bottom end, two mattresses had been thrown horizontally on the floor beneath the broken air conditioner, plastered on the wall opposite the inner bathroom door. A pile of backpacks rested on the table by the glass window, which was blinded by an old white lace cloth.

If the messy and ill-equipped room was a representation of all the hotel's rooms, then the customers did not care. They kept coming in their numbers.

Ella's mother said, "Welcome again. Make yourselves comfortable. At least for now, while my roommates are out and about."

"Oh, you do have roommates. I was about to ask if you came with all these bags." Claudia sat on the bed with Ella and her mother.

"My dear, everyone here has a roommate. The island is crowded. In fact, it is so congested that the locals are converting sections of their family houses into hotels."

"For real?" Kingsley said from where he sat on the floor.

"Yes! For real. About a hundred migrants arrive here daily. It's crazy."

"Wait, did you say migrants? We thought they were tourists!" Kingsley said with a laugh.

Claudia said, "Exactly! But, you know, I did doubt a little when I saw Africans. Initially, I'd thought they were natives, but then I heard them speak French."

"Ha! Are you saying Africans don't tour?" Kingsley asked.

"Exactly the question on my mind," Ella's mother added.

"Come on, you know what I mean. Of course, they do tour, but I'm certain not many Africans know of this island. We saw a great number of them on our way up here," Claudia said.

Hassan and Bara came back from reception, where they'd gone to secure a room for the group.

"We got the last room on the third floor," Bara said as they slumped on the mattress by Kingsley.

"Guess what? All these people we thought were tourists are actually just migrants like us," Kingsley said.

Ella's mother said, "Well, not all. Maybe 95 percent. The island does receive tourists. I've met a few at the restaurants, but they all stay at the classic hotels reserved for them, by the shore. I remember the first day I arrived. All the hotels were full except for those by the shore. Nevertheless, they turned me away."

"Even with empty rooms? Those people are not business minded," Claudia concluded.

"It's their policy. Besides, those hotels are awfully expensive. I could not have afforded two nights!"

"So how did you find this place?" Hassan asked.

"Oh, I eventually became tired and hungry. I found a restaurant to rest and feed my child. Ella, stop manipulating my phone!"

Ella kept rolling from one side of the bed to the next with the phone.

"Let the poor girl be. She must have been through a lot," Claudia said.

"She keeps watching the same cartoon video repeatedly. The battery will soon drain out, and electricity here is on and off."

"And so is the signal. You won't need the phone. Let her play," Claudia insisted.

"You know, you're actually right about the signal. Anyway, like I was saying, I met my roommate Cynthia at the restaurant. A Ghanaian girl whom I help with a pen. I opened up to her, and she brought me here. I've met lots of other Africans."

"You see! It is good to be good," Claudia proclaimed.

"Talking about restaurants, can we find one? I need a plate of some local delicacy. Perhaps two plates. I'm starving," Bara confessed.

"What you need is some exercise. You eat too much," Claudia said.

"Are you trying to call me fat? You just said it was good to be good. That is not being good!" Bara responded playfully.

"Bro, she carries your weight every other night. How do you think she feels?" Hassan laughed as he rose.

"No way!" Ella's mother said.

"Yep way," Kingsley replied.

"Shut up, Kingsley" Claudia joked.

"What can I say? I come in full," Bara said.

"You know, at the border, I wanted to tell you that you both sounded like a love story in the making when you argued" Ella's mother recalled.

"You have no idea!" Hassan said.

"Oh my God! Can everyone just stop? There's a child in the room!" Claudia yelled, laughing as they all exited the room.

"OK, you guys go freshen up. I will too—and then we'll go have lunch," Ella's mother said.

"All right, dear, we'll be down in twenty minutes," Claudia assured.

• • • • • • • • ● ○○○○○○○○○ ○ ○

By the immigration building, a camerawoman was filming two men who appeared to be having a conversation.

"Who are they?" Bara asked.

"I have no idea. Probably some tourists or a news channel," Ella's mother replied.

"So, we're basically a nongovernmental organization that is here with hopes of talking to a few migrants," one of the men said as the migrants walked past them and entered the restaurant.

"Hello! Good morning."

"Good morning. How are you today?" Ella's mother and the waitress exchanged greetings in Spanish.

"Not bad at all. Wow! I see you've been learning some Español!" Hassan said.

"You bet I have," Ella's mother boasted.

"Mom! I want bread and chocolate," Ella said when she saw a little boy leaving the restaurant with bread and chocolate.

"Sure, little mama, but you'll have to save it for later," her mother replied, and then she asked the waiter for plates of rice and chicken.

Claudia was looking on her phone and retouching her lipstick. She didn't even notice that one of the guys at the opposite end could not keep his eyes off her.

"How did you find yourself here?" Kingsley asked before gulping down some of the island's fresh water. "This is so good" He commended.

"I'd gone for a business trip, but I decided to stay in Nigeria after I heard that the war back home had intensified. Then when they began extraditing us to Cameroon, I packed and left Nigeria in fear. Next thing I know, I'm standing on an island, buying rubber boots from its local shop and embarking on a journey to America."

The waitress brought their plates and went back for a second round.

"America!" they said, almost in a chorus.

"Come on, you traveled all this way? And you experienced firsthand how difficult and dangerous it's been. People and even the police take advantage of you, especially if you can't express yourself in their language."

"Trust me, you're preaching to the choir," Kingsley said.

"I'd arranged to leave this morning, but I had to change plans. Cynthia told me that the Cuban guy asking her out had said that someone had said that there's another section of the ocean from here that will reduce about three of your days in the jungle," Ella's mother said.

"And you believed him? That's a lot of hearsay!" Claudia said.

"We did. He has no reason to lie. He's coming with us anyway. Let me tell you, the jungle is rough and dreadful. I've heard horrifying things happen in there. My friend and I both have kids. The water I've been told, is equally not the safest, but right now, the shorter road is safer for us."

"This rice is so good," Hassan said.

"It is. I might need a second plate," Bara responded.

"Really?" Claudia said, and they all laughed.

"What? Haven't you heard we'll be crossing jungles? Eat for your own good," Bara said as they laughed.

"Sincerely, I had no idea about a jungle" Hassan confessed. "This journey gets crazier every day."

"Ha! We had no idea about anything. Just roaming about like a bunch of lost cattle," Kingsley responded.

"I know!" Claudia said.

"Anyway, when do you leave?" Hassan asked.

"Tomorrow. Early in the morning," Ella's mother replied.

Hassan turned and looked at his friends curiously.

"Nope!"

"No!"

"Don't even think it!"

"What! I didn't even say anything," Hassan said with a laugh.

"You said a lot, bro. I don't ever want anything to do with water again. I don't even want to learn how to swim anymore," Bara said.

"Ha! I'm even terrified of drinking," Kingsley confessed.

"I don't blame you. After all those hard drops, I'm pretty sure my menses will come sooner."

"Ew!"

"Seriously?"

"Oh my God! I was literally eating."

"What?" Claudia laughed with Ella's mother. She retouched her lipstick after the last spoonful of rice. She still had not noticed the secret admirer who had remained fixed on her, sipping lemonade and perhaps planning his move. His irritating presence evoked something covetous in Bara, and he wanted so badly to let him know that she was taken, but he did not. He thought he'd look desperate.

"So, where are the girls you share the room with? I need my queens around. I'm tired of these boys. One can't express her mind in peace," Claudia said with a smile.

Ella's mother kept laughing nonstop. "I swear, you are one crazy, sweet girl. Well, they are not only girls. They went to buy their boots and food. They'll leave tomorrow morning."

"Guys! Let's leave with them. It'll be safer to be in a larger group," Kingsley said.

"What? We're now going to America? That's like a billion miles and a dozen countries from here. No, I'll stay in any country that lets me," Bara said.

"Then you'll stay there alone. Look, I've heard Hassan speak Spanish, and I can assure you that I will never understand that language," Kingsley said provoking laughter yet again. "I'm sorry. I have a hard time with languages. Its reasons why I spoke late, my mother tells me."

"And you sure haven't stopped speaking since then. It's hard to believe that you spoke late. You talk too much." Hassan laughed as they paid the bill, bought Ella bread and chocolate, and went to check on Aadesh at the health center.

• • • • • • • • ● ○○○○○○○ ○ ○ ○

Bara had wished for an endless night, but that was never going to happen. He couldn't tell what annoyed him more: the short night or the footsteps and voices in the hotel that woke him up. "I just don't understand why we must leave so early. We didn't have enough sleep."

"Ha! We had enough sleep, especially you. You weren't even awake when Ella's mother came to say goodbye," Hassan said.

"Thank God. That sounded sad," Bara replied.

"It was, but we'll see them ahead," Claudia said as they joined a group of other Africans downstairs.

They advanced tentatively to the end of the road that left the island. As they walked, they became more and more serene.

"Let's gather for a word of prayer," Frank said. From that day on, he would be referred to as Pastor.

They stood in their rainboots, each with a backpack of supplies, a machete, and a portable tent, staring in wonder at the footpath that ran up the steep hill, coated by the dreadful jungle of the perilous Darien Gap. And although the sun had risen defyingly and the day looked promising, all they really saw was uncertainty.

"Now, let's pray. Dear God," Pastor began.

CHAPTER 9

CYNTHIA AND ELLA'S mother stood among dozens of others. Their babies with them, gazing into the still night, with a silence fortified by the rumbling waters.

"Lord, have mercy," Ella's mother mumbled as she counted her steps to the boat, her heart saying no, and her mind saying yes. For a moment, she agreed with her heart, and she considered a retreat. *To what and where?* She thought. She looked back into the opaque night and remembered the expired five-day permit in her bag and knew that she had no other option.

"Something is wrong, Jose," Cynthia whispered to her boyfriend.

Jose was a good man with a heavy build. He acquired his muscles from working construction back in Cuba, but he never mentioned where he'd learned to speak English so well.

"What's wrong?" He used a piece of cloth to tie Cynthia's eight-year-old to him, and then he did same to Ella and her mother. It was how they'd crossed the ocean the first time. That way, they were able to hold on to the boat, both for themselves and the kids.

Cynthia said, "First, the captains said we'll only sail when it's dark because, according to them, the waters will be safer at night. So, we waited here all day, though he would not tell us why that was. Now, they're telling us to shush like they're scared someone is listening."

Ella's mother responded, "And have you realized the two boats have no lighting? How do they intend to navigate the ocean in darkness? Oh my God! Life jackets. They haven't supplied us with life jackets,"

"Exactly!" Cynthia agreed.

"You might be right," Jose said.

"Life jackets! Life jackets!" they called as the captains took off carelessly, one after the other.

In the two boats, were Africans, Asians, and a few Central Americans, mainly Cubans and Haitians. Lies, they would have said, had anyone told them there was a deadlier part of the ocean than the first one they'd experienced. Those waters had been ravaging, but these were devouring and deadly.

The two boats skimmed at dizzying speeds, overcoming ghastly waves that had become more frequent with increasing distance. It seemed like the captains knew what they were doing as they maneuvered skillfully across the perilous waters like seasoned sailors.

Ella's mother and her friends were in the second boat, trailing the first by a few hundred feet. Suddenly, their boat decelerated and stopped. The deep groaning sound of the engine changed to a rattle, and it swayed from side to side as the ocean pushed against it. "What's happening?" she asked.

"We've had an engine failure," Jose translated after the captain.

"We're finished!" Cynthia declared.

There was no telling how far offshore they had gone. All that surrounded them were endless miles of water, threatening and dreadful, and ready to suck them in at the slightest mistake.

In oblivion, the first captain skimmed away into obscurity, leaving his partner behind to deal with the grumbles, the curses, and the insults that were being fired at him from all across the boat.

"I want to pee," a girl said from the back. Nobody, not even the mother, gave her any attention.

"Oh my God!"

A huge wave was rolling unwaveringly toward them. The migrants held on as strongly as they could to any part of the boat they could grab. The captain had abandoned his position at the back and sat among the migrants for his own safety.

In a second, the malevolent wave hit the boat and pushed it mercilessly to instability. It slanted and nearly collected water, but it wiggled back up and then wobbled uncontrollably as the wave passed along.

"Oh, I should have known! Someone should have told me this was a bad idea. My children! My wife!" a man cried.

Those seated on the sides put their arms into the water and paddled to keep the boat stable, but even that was of very little help.

Babies began crying, and adults launched prayers, binding and casting, rebuking and rejecting, all in the name of Jesus.

"Lord, have pity," Ella's mother pleaded.

"What's wrong, Mama?" Cynthia's son whispered.

"Nothing, Papi. Don't worry. We'll leave soon, OK?" her boyfriend said.

"Lord, have mercy," Ella's mother begged again, fighting back tears. It had only been a couple of months since she had lost the love of her life and became a widow at twenty-nine. And here she was at night with their daughter in the middle of an ocean. Their fate was in limbo and their entire lives depended on a failed boat to keep their heads above the water. She looked down at her innocent daughter, her arms wrapped tightly around her, and for a moment, she regretted bringing her into this unfortunate world—a place so unfair that bad things happened to good people like her dad.

"Who has a knife?" Jose yelled to translate the captain's perturbing question.

"A knife? What could he possibly want with a knife?" Cynthia asked nervously.

It was hard not to imagine the worst. After all, they were stuck in the middle of an ocean with a man they knew nothing about—and they had entrusted their lives in his hands. A few people had their phones with them and switched on their flashlights. But it was night, and the ocean was vast and vacant. Flashlights would not stop anyone from doing anything.

From where he sat on the last bench, the captain crawled to the motor at the rear of the boat. Someone had given him a nail cutter, and he managed to untie and retie a few screws. He tried to restart the motor.

The engine rattled for a few minutes. The curses, insults, and prayers grew louder as more waves attacked them. The captain adjusted a few screws and tried again.

Finally, the engine kicked off and sent them skimming again.

"Thank God!" they shouted.

After several miles, blinding lights flashed over them from behind. A sophisticated boat was advancing with a threatening speed. They were being followed, but the captain sped up. Pushing the boat to its limits, it now felt like it flew over the waters.

Babies cried and clung to their mothers. Prayers resumed and the insults followed, but they changed nothing. Another deadly wave approached as the captain flee from the military boat chasing them.

• • • • • • • • ⬤ ○○○○○○○○ ○ ○

A thick dark forest spread gently across endless hectares. The first boat had just harbored, and the migrants were scrambling for their bags.

Boom! Boom! Boom! A Panamanian military boat patrolling the shores, fired gunshots into the air as it sped toward them. In fear and trepidation, they took off into the dark jungle, scattering in different directions. Some left behind their bags, and others grabbed bags that weren't theirs. The bullet spray continued, sounding closer each time.

"Solange! Solange!" Sema called anxiously. He turned around as if to head back to the shore.

"Where do you think you're going?" Gilbert asked.

"My wife, bro! My wife! She's pregnant. What if she got hit?"

"Bro … hey … hey! Listen to me," Gilbert said.

"Oh God! What kind of man am I?" Sema asked, panicking.

"There's nothing you can do right now. We have to—"

The gunshots intensified, and it sounded like the shooters were just a few feet away.

They hid behind a large tree and listened in horror, trying their best to breathe quietly.

The officers approached with shotguns and headlamps. They'd apprehended two migrants. They searched meticulously as they walked. Their bright lights revealed every nook and cranny of the jungle. It didn't take much effort to find Sema and Gilbert. They were taken to the military boat with the other two captives and whisked away.

• • • • • • • • ⬤ ○○○○○○○○ ○ ○

In the second boat, they were shouting as they sped, escaping endless gunshots from the military behind them. Then, the boat collided with the gigantic wave and was tossed high in the air.

With the hysteria in the boat and the military behind him, the captain lost control. The boat spun and tilted in the air and landed on its side. There were desperate cries and deafening screams as it surged and emptied its contents into the ravaging ocean, which was determined to swallow them all in minutes. Cries for help filled the air as they flapped in the water in hopeless attempts to swim.

As a Cuban, Jose was no stranger to water. He'd grown up swimming in the ocean for leisure. So, even though the present situation required extraordinary skills, he managed to keep his head and that of the child tied to him above the water.

The military officers in life jackets dashed into the water. They rescued a few people after a long struggle, including Jose and Cynthia's child, but the majority were gone, including Cynthia, Ella's mother and little Ella.

CHAPTER 10

CLAUDIA, LIKE THE rest, had always believed that Africa was the only place on the planet with hills like mountains, but how wrong had they been. They creeped up the endless rocky hill, insulting and cursing their political leaders back home.

"I can't," Linda said as she slumped down and began unloading her bag. She threw away a few clothes, cans of sardines, soft drinks, and liquid milk. Even the big yellow Good News Bible had to go. "I'm sorry God, but I can't … I just can't. The bag is too heavy."

"I feel you. I already threw away my machete and a few of my clothes," Kingsley responded, slumping by her to take a breath.

They had decided to greatly reduce the intensities of their flashlights. The stories they'd heard back on the island, hinted those lights in the jungle at night were not a good idea. It could attract attention—the wrong kind. From wild animals to robbers and traffickers, the incidents were real, and reoccurrences were hugely possible.

"Let's keep moving," Pastor said. He'd more or less assumed the leadership position. Perhaps it was because he'd managed to convince everyone that the journey was just as spiritually demanding as it was physically or because he was tall and muscular.

"Can we rest a little longer? I need to catch my breath," said a guy from Guinea in French.

Hassan and a few other Cameroonians translated it into English.

Pastor insisted that the rest was over. "We can't afford long rests. We have a long way to go." He butchered and arranged a young tree into a walking stick for the Guinean.

They proceeded strenuously up the hill, reaching out for stones, trees, roots, and anything else they could get a hold of for support.

It began thundering.

"God, please! I cannot take this right now," someone said.

"That sound reminds me of you Hassan," Kingsley said, provoking Bara and Claudia into laughter.

"Bro, how come you no longer fart like you used to?" Bara asked.

"Shut up. It depends on what I eat," Hassan replied playfully.

"What's going on? Please keep your voices down. There's no telling what or who might hear you," Pastor said.

"Hmmm finally!" Linda said as the hill gradually leveled up. They'd arrived at the top, and the Guinean guy trailed the group.

Pastor wanted to continue, but he had to agree that it was arduous to advance in that state of inadequate light. They decided to spend the night on the hilltop. They had each bought a tent, but they agreed to sleep in groups, which was safer. They set up a few tents, and even though it wasn't the most comfortable space to sleep, it did keep them dry from the rains that trickled down through the thick trees.

· · · · · · · · ● ○○○○○○○○ ○ ○

It was barely dawn, and a few birds were already whistling. The migrants were folding up their tents. A few of them brushed their teeth, but the others did not care. They started down the steep hill. The rain had left the ground muddy and slippery, and for every step they took, they had to hold a tree.

Linda decided to scoot down the hill between the trees, but Claudia wanted to stay as clean as she could. Besides, Bara had taken her bag. He'd said that he had no excuses. He wanted to step up and be a man, and the jungle was an opportunity for him to prove that he'd always be available—even in difficult times. If he had to be entirely honest, his civility had been greatly inspired by jealousy from seeing other men admire her and make moves at her. *The nerve of that one guy who actually came up to ask her for her number at the hotel on the island.*

It took hours, but they finally made it down the hill. They proceeded to cross a stream, and they rested on the stunningly large whitish granite rocks.

"I wonder how Aadesh is doing," Hassan said.

"Me too. I kinda miss them," Claudia replied.

"I'm sorry, but I'm looking around, and all I can see are the stunning and fatiguing hills we have to ascend and descend. That's all I'm thinking about right now," Bara said.

"How selfish! But I feel you though," Hassan responded.

They continued chitchatting as they ate biscuits, bread, chocolates, and sardines. They would share, if necessary, but for convenience, they ate mostly out of their own bags.

"God knows I need some roasted fish right now!" Pastor said.

"You have no idea," Isa, the tall, glittering ebony-skinned South Sudanese, replied as he and Pastor stood by the stream and watched the fish swimming carelessly.

"We need to keep going," Pastor said as they returned to the group. The sun had come up, and so had the heat. They knew it was dangerous and onerous to navigate the jungle by night. So, they were determined to cover as much distance as possible during the day.

They picked up their bags and walked on the lovely but uncomfortable pebbles, through the withering elephant grass, and across a vast brownish field.

Bara was right. At the edge of the field, a hill ascended sharply into the air, completely blanketed by a massive forest that truly, was a sparkling dark green on the outside but dull and deadly on the inside.

· · · · · · · · ● ○○○○○○○○ ○ ○

"Shush! I heard something," Solange said.

"I thought so too. Gilbert!" Vera called.

"Shush! What if it's not him?" Solange pulled her behind a tree.

"You're right. We might attract the wrong attention," Vera whispered.

Solange and Vera were lost in the jungle. Unfortunately, the previous night's saga had separated their group. In a desperate attempt for safety, they'd ran mindlessly into the jungle in different directions, and she'd ended up with Vera, a fellow migrant friend from Uganda. Good thing they'd known each other back on the island. They stood deathly silent behind a tree that was large enough to completely hide Solange's five-month pregnancy.

"Maybe it was just an animal," Solange said after a few minutes.

"Maybe it was. Doesn't make me feel any better though. Have you any idea what type of animals might live in here?"

"Of course, Vera. I watch Animal Planet," Solange replied as they stepped out cautiously.

"Where could have everyone run to? My God, how will we survive without food? Look at my condition." Solange was fighting back tears.

"You have to be strong, my sister, but how come you and Sema ran in different directions?" Vera asked.

"I don't know! Everything happened so fast." Solange replied.

"You're right. It did."

They sat hopelessly behind the huge tree, guessing and second-guessing their every decision. Through the short distance they'd walked since morning, they'd noticed a few water bottles and biscuit and candy packages thrown by the side of the narrow footpath. It indicated that others had used the road, and they believed they were on the right path.

They decided to stay where they were. They were on the right path, and sooner or later, someone was going to find them.

"But what if they're already ahead?" Vera asked.

"Trust me. I know my husband. Sema will not go anywhere without me," Solange said.

"Yeah, but what if he's searching for you ahead? We'd be waiting in vain. We need to start going," Vera said.

"How about we return to the shore? See if the boat is still there. We might retrieve our bags," Solange suggested.

"That's hardly going to be fruitful. What if the police are still there? What if the captain came back and took his boat away?"

"I saw that man take off into the jungle. Trust me, he's never going back to that place. Not even for the boat."

"I'm just saying. It'll be worse if we return to danger, or nothing at all, and have to walk back all the way" Vera said.

· · · · · · · · ● ○○○○○○○○ ○ ○

Elsewhere, not too far from Solange and Vera, another group of migrants was lost and confused.

"Crying is not going to help you or the situation at hand, Emilda," Ali said.

"It's been hours of endless wandering in the woods. I'm tired!" Emilda complained as she leaned against a tree.

"We all are, but we need to keep going," Ali proposed.

"Going where, Ali? Where exactly are we going? We've been roaming about this jungle for hours. I think an hour of rest is OK," Kamali, a fellow Ethiopian, yelled.

"And I've been here, roaming with you. So, put down your voice, bro. I'm not the reason we're lost," Ali stated.

"I'm sorry … whatever," Kamali said after a moment of awkward silence.

"What do you mean *whatever*?" Ali asked, mildly irritated.

"Ali is right. We need to keep going," Kofi said from where he'd stood in regrets. "I don't know about you, but I'll only truly rest after we've found a path."

"Thank you! That's exactly what I was trying to say," Ali said.

They continued across the jungle, battling insect bites, thirst, and hunger that would have been worse had Kofi not grabbed a bag before fleeing the unexpected scandal at the shore. And even though he'd realized the bag wasn't his and didn't have water or energy candy, they still were grateful to have shared the two packets of biscuits and bread he'd found in it. Beneath the food, he'd also found a few clothes and a pair of shoes, which they ignored.

They were almost giving up to rest, when Emilda saw a dirty piece of red cloth, tied around a tree.

Kamali whispered, "I suggest we run. Let's walk in a different direction. Why is a piece of cloth tied around a tree in the middle of the jungle?"

"I think we should take a closer look," Ali said.

"Of course you do," Kamali responded sarcastically.

"What is your problem with Ali?" Kofi asked.

"What is your problem with me?" Kamali whispered harshly. "There's a piece of cloth, red in color, and tied around a tree. Has it occurred to you even for a second that there could be a gang here—and that is probably a mark for their territory?"

"Bro, I don't know what the beef is between you both, but he has a point. What he just said makes some sense," Kofi said.

"OK, you guys, wait here. I'll go see what it is," Ali said.

"I'll go with you," Emilda opted and followed Ali.

"Of course, you will," Kamali murmured.

"Bro, you have to let it go," Kofi said.

"What?" Kamali asked.

"Come on. I'm not a kid. It has something to do with the girl. Anyway, I don't know about you, but I'm not about to stand back while a woman has summoned the courage to explore something potentially dangerous" Kofi said as he left.

"Oh please! She only went because Ali did," Kamali replied and followed reluctantly.

"Yes! Yes! It's a path," Ali said.

"Yes, it is. Thank God. Come on!" Emilda called.

"Shush! We're still in here. Bring down your voices," Kamali enjoined.

After hours of unproductive searching, they were finally standing on a narrow footpath that curved up the hill.

"The cloth is probably just an indication of the road by other road users," Emilda said.

"Don't get too excited. Could still be leading us straight into a den of bandits," Kamali responded as they followed the group up the hill.

They descended to a stunning greenish plane that was punctuated by little bush trees.

Emilda spread out her arms. "Goodness! How satisfying to finally feel the sun on my skin again."

"I know, right? God, I was beginning to feel claustrophobic," Kofi responded. "Wow!" He took off immediately.

To their left, there were a few guava trees with a good quantity of the ripe fruit. They sped toward the tree, not caring that the birds had begun feasting on some of the fruit. They ate and filled the bag.

"Honestly, these guavas are a lifesaver. I don't know for how much longer I'd have gone before passing out," Kamali said. "OK, I'm going to say it. I was wrong about the road."

"That must have been difficult for you to admit," Ali said sarcastically.

"What do you think?" Kamali replied.

They advanced across the field. Toward the end, by a quiet stream, two women were drinking out of their hands.

"Solange! Oh my God, Solange," Emilda called.

"Emilda!" Solange called back.

"Finally, we see human beings," Vera said as they all ran into each other's arms.

"Here, have some guavas." Kofi offered them the bag.

"Jesus! You're a lifesaver. Where did you find them?"

They ate like wild beasts.

"Hidden over there in the bushes."

"You must have missed it." Kofi and Kamali rushed to drink from the crystal-clear stream.

"I can't find Sema. I thought he must have run off with you," Solange said.

"No, he didn't. The shooting was unanticipated. We must have run in different directions, but not to worry, I'm sure we'll find them—or they'll find us soon," Ali said.

"I hope so. I'm beginning to have this strange feeling," Solange admitted sadly.

"Don't. He's well. I promise you," Ali said as he joined the rest for a drink.

Kofi had only met them on the boat. The rest of them had all lived in the same hotel and known each other during their few days on the island. And even though Ali and Kamali were Ethiopians, Emilda and Solange were from Cameroon, Kofi and Vera were from Ghana and Uganda respectively, they all found an even stronger bond under one identity: Africans.

CHAPTER 11

A **LOUD TRILL INTERRUPTED** the death silence that had loomed over them for hours. Bara swore it was a chimpanzee. He had once watched a documentary, and though no one fully believed him, it still gave them quite the scare. None of them was precisely sure what it was—and Bara could have been right.

Inspired by that frightening probability, they attempted to speed up, but the hill was perilously stony, steep, and crisscrossed by thick roots. It seemed to level, and after a minute or two of effortless walk, it rose again, slanting into the air and into the enveloping massive trees that provided shade from the scorching sun, but also trapping and cornering.

Kingsley looked around, but all he saw were brownish decaying leaves beneath trees. He remembered a time when all they saw was water. Now, he couldn't tell which experience he despised more.

As usual, the guy from Guinee trailed the group down the hill. "To be honest, he is slowing us down. How can these girls be faster than you, bro?" Pastor asked.

"Come on, people are different," Hassan said. "Just add a little effort. This is probably our last hill to climb."

They all agreed, but how wrong they were. It leveled and sloped up again. They were unaware of the undulations of about seven other hills cascading before them, and they didn't know that for the rest of the day, they'd only imagine the skies, but not see it, and hear the winds whisper far up through the tree branches, but not feel it.

"I can't," Linda cried out a few minutes up the next hill.

"Yeah! Let's rest."

"Bro! What's going on?" they asked randomly.

The Guinean guy leaned weakly against a tree, his hand on his chest, as he fought for air. He staggered to the ground, wheezing audibly as he tried to get air into his lungs.

"He's having an asthma attack," Linda said as she rushed to the scene. "Spray! Spray! Where is your spray?"

He pointed weakly to his backpack, and they hurriedly found the inhaler. He placed it in his mouth and inhaled it steadily until the wheezing finally stopped.

"Do you feel OK? Do you want some water?"

They decided to take a rest on his behalf.

"Have you been asthmatic for long, bro?" Hassan asked.

Twenty-five minutes was enough for everyone to refill their energy and for the Guinean to recuperate.

"Yeah, I've suffered from it since I was young, but it felt different this time. It felt like a combination of asthma and something else ... maybe panic."

"I see. That's understandable. I'm Hassan, by the way."

"I'm Solomon—and thanks for helping out."

"Of course, bro. You're welcome. Just do your best to keep up," Hassan said as they trailed behind the group.

"Is it just me or does anyone smell something?" Claudia asked.

"Yeah! I do. I was just about to ask."

A rank and sickening smell was gradually intensifying as they approached the hilltop. They were constantly spitting and cupped their hands over their noses.

"I think I'm going to vomit," Bara said.

"What is that?" Kingsley pointed into the woods.

A dead man sat beneath a tree, decaying in the open like an animal. His bag pack was by him, and a half-drunk water bottle had fallen out of his saggy hand. His eyes were open, and his head, tilted over his shoulder. His skin was almost colorless and countless flies and other insects gallivanted nonstop around him as he sat, decomposing faster than the clothes he wore.

"Oh, Jesus!" Linda said.

"What a pity. That is a human being!" They tried to keep the pungent smell away from their noses.

Claudia could not help herself. The scene had broken her to the core.

For those who knew her, it was terrifying to see her in that state. She wasn't one to be broken easily.

They stood some distance away from the smell, pondering a million questions: What could have killed him? Did he lose hope and give up? Did he get sick? Maybe he got bitten by a snake. They were in the Darien jungle after all. Who will report of his death? Had he left a family back home? Are they waiting in vain for a call that will never come?

"That's all right. That's OK." Bara put a hand on Claudia's back.

"Guys I don't think we're ready for this journey," Claudia said as they slowly left with the poignant image imprinted in their minds, perhaps forever.

In silence, they descended a short slope and embarked on the next hill.

Solomon still lagged behind, but he was close enough to be seen. He couldn't help but feel guilty when the group had to stop and wait for him. *Maybe they would go faster without me. Maybe they actually have a chance of getting out of this jungle earlier if they just forget about me and move on. The footpath seems clear. I will follow behind at my own pace.* He remembered the corpse and quickly changed his mind. *Nope! This jungle is not safe, and I'm already handicapped by asthma. If anything must happen to me, at least let there be someone around to tell the story. I'll do my best to keep up, and I'll beg for a rest when I cannot continue. Yeah! And I'll keep begging if I have to until I make it. I've come so far. I can finish this.* The thoughts of encouragement had inspired an influx of courage that boosted his energy and made him believe that he could.

"I don't know which one I hate more, ascending or descending these hills," Isa said as they arrived yet another hilltop and waited for Solomon to catch up.

"Honestly, at this point, I just hate everything," Claudia responded. "I hate that I haven't seen the sky or felt the wind since this morning. I hate that I'm here, that anyone is here, going through this. I even hate these leaves. Leaves! Leaves! Leaves everywhere."

"You need to calm down," Pastor said.

"Calm down?" Claudia asked, slightly raising her voice. "We just saw a man rotting beneath a tree like a leaf and walked on by like it didn't mean a thing. Even worse, we don't even know what killed him. We could be walking right into our own doom."

"What did you want us to do?" Pastor asked.

"I don't know! Pray, lay a branch on him, or something … you are the pastor, you tell me," Claudia responded.

Pastor replied, "Please! My name is Frank, and I don't remember stopping anyone from doing anything."

"Guys, calm down. To be honest, we still have a long way to go, and I feel we might have to deal with more devastating situations. Everyone needs to put themselves together" Bara said.

"Exactly! It was traumatizing to see, but there was nothing we could do to change the situation. We need to focus on us for now." Pastor started down the hill.

They all followed in an awkward silence as they descended nonstop, depending on the trees and roots for stability. Any missed step on the steep hill could lead to fatal consequences.

The hill finished in a marshy valley that hosted every breed of mosquito in the world.

A sharp hissing sound sounded out from the grass. They may have doubted the trills they'd heard in the morning, but they knew for certain what this came from.

"Guys!" Kingsley started stepping back slowly.

"Shush!" Isa said.

"It's over for us," Kingsley declared.

An anaconda was submerged in the still water.

"Stand still—and don't say a word," Pastor whispered.

"Shouldn't we just run?" Linda asked as she held tightly to Isa's arm.

"I don't think that's a good idea."

"Let's be quiet please."

"I'm sure it runs faster."

"It's in water."

"Yeah, but it can also come on land."

"Quiet please! If it perceives attack, it will retaliate—and we'll be doomed." Pastor said.

Kingsley whispered "So, what? We're just going to stand here until it starts eating us up one after the other?"

They froze as the beast lifted its monstrous head.

Kingsley began saying his last prayer.

"Oh my God. It's moving. It's moving," Claudia whispered.

The creature began swimming toward the opposite end of the swamp. It slithered out and disappeared into the thick green bush.

Kingsley took off like an antelope fleeing a lion, and they took off right behind him. Despite how difficult it was to run through the woods, they only stopped when the footpath sloped up another hill.

"I just saw an anaconda! My God, Bara! I just saw an anaconda! What's next?" Kingsley asked between heavy breaths.

"Bro, you need to exercise calm in situations like these," Pastor said.

"Yeah! A snake would only attack you if it felt attacked," Hassan responded.

Kingsley said, "Calm? So, why did you run after me then? That thing could swallow Bara in one gulp—and he's twice my size. Do you know what that means for me?"

"Really!" Bara commented.

"No offense, bro. Look, I don't know about you guys, but I have an immense phobia about snakes. I'd rather meet a lion" Kingsley confessed.

They took a few minutes to catch their breath.

Solomon had pleaded for more time, but they had to leave. The snake was still in the vicinity, the sun had also begun setting, and the evening cold was slowly taking over.

• • • • • • • • ● ○○○○○○○○ ○ ○

A field of fine golden sand slept lavishly between a little forest and a dark lake. The sun finally disappeared behind the hilly jungle, and the quiet of the night sunk in.

Ali, Kofi and Kamali rested on the sand and some branches. Kamali was talking nonstop and getting cozy with Vera to avoid Ali and to provoke Emilda's jealousy.

She didn't fall for it. She chose the guy she chose for a reason, and even back on the island, where they'd argued and almost fought over her, she'd made Kamali understand in the most amicable and respectful of ways that he wasn't the one. Her heart had found more interest in Ali. It was not that Kamali was a bad person, but her heart just wanted what it wanted.

Kamali refused to give up. He was sure Emilda felt something for him and thought Ali did not deserve her. He would have treated her better.

They slept through the night. Besides the brown frogs that came out of the water and hopped on their legs, it was otherwise serene and peaceful.

When the night was over, they were up and on their feet. They ascended and descended for miles on nothing but stream water and guavas, which were now finished. And though they were yet to see anything remotely close to human settlement, they took comfort in the thought that it was their last day in the jungle, according to the stories they'd heard back on the island.

There were still miles to cover, and Vera could no longer depend on her legs. She was a curvy girl, and her underwear was doing her no good. "Ice! I need ice," she said. The friction between her legs had yielded scorching and unendurable bruises. She had fallen and could no longer rise. The pain was intolerable.

"Spread your legs." Emilda started to take off her pants.

"OK! I think it's time for us to leave," Kofi said, provoking some laughter.

"Oh, were you waiting to be told?" Solange asked sarcastically as the guys left and stood a distance away.

"I can't continue," Vera said.

"You can and you have to. You have to try," Solange said.

"No, you'll have to go ahead. I can't keep up with the speed." She was fighting back tears.

"So what? You'll be out here in the wild all by yourself? That is a suicide mission! Dear, look at me," Solange said. "I've made it this far. Do you think it's been easy for me, especially without Sema? Come on, you have to find a way to keep trying. This is no place for anyone to be alone."

The bruises were severe, and blood had begun to trickle out from a few. They did not know for sure that it would help, but Solange and Emilda found a few grasses that looked similar to the traditional ones used back home to inhibit bleeding. Vera screamed in agony as they squeezed the juice onto the wounds and then waited for the pain to subside.

Not that it was OK to laugh, but when Vera had finally gotten up and walked like both her legs hated each other, Kamali could not get a hold of himself. It was a sad, funny moment as they walked across the stony field.

A group of about thirty Cubans approached them from behind.

"Hola, amigos!" the Cubans called as they passed ahead.

"Amigos!" the Africans called back.

Rumors were that all Cubans, especially the males, had been mandated to serve in the Cuban military for a year. The jungle was a tough experience for them, but they seemed to handle it with disproportionate ease.

"Why are they all gathered around? What's going on?" Ali asked as they approached the scene in wonder.

A dead Cuban couple was in the center. Dried blood that had been browned by the sun trailed into the ground from the bullet hole in the man's hip. His wife was on her stomach, and her pants and underwear were off. Her sacredness had been desecrated. Her pride had been devoured and left exposed shamelessly to anything and anyone in the wild. Their clothes and bags had been scattered, and a torn wallet had been left by their garments. Their identity cards had been tossed a few feet away by the wind.

"It must have been recent," Ali said.

They pondered one theory and the next, but they always landed on the most apparent. A gang must have robbed them and raped the woman, and the man must have been shot attempting to protect his wife.

They put the clothes on the woman then left a few branches over them and went on their way.

It was dangerous for anyone to navigate the jungle alone. Vera was now determined more than ever to tag along with the group, despite her excruciating wounds. She and her African friends did their best to keep up, but it wasn't long before the Cubans were out of sight.

CHAPTER 12

UNFORTUNATELY, IT WAS impossible to complete the hills in a day, and they spent the night on top of one. They heard a river roaring at the foot of the hill they were now descending. They had long ago exhausted their water and depended on soft drinks to quench their thirst—but no other liquid could do the job like water. They hurried down the hill with great excitement.

"Bro," a weary voice said when Kingsley stopped.

"Hello. What are you doing here all by yourself?" Kingsley asked.

His friends came out right after him, and they all surrounded the Indian man who sat helpless in the shade of the trees that grew over the stream.

"They gave up on me," he said, pointing to his feet, which were swollen. His soles were plastered with blisters and open sores. Flies covered the scarlet sores. "Have you met any other Indians on your way?"

"Unfortunately, no," Pastor answered.

"But why did you set out alone, my friend?" Bara asked.

"I did not. I was with a friend, but he gave up after the first hill and went back to the island. So, I had to continue on my own."

"Sorry to hear," Linda said.

"We had no idea it would be this difficult and dangerous." He pleaded for water after explaining how painful and laborious it was to crawl to the stream for a drink.

Claudia and Linda went to fetch water in the juice containers, and Hassan lowered his bag and took out a few first aid implements he'd bought on the island. He cleaned the man's feet with a piece of cloth that Claudia soaked with water.

"Hold him please," Hassan said to Pastor and Solomon.

The man screamed as Hassan disinfected the wounds with alcohol from a dark green bottle.

"Thank you, brothers. God bless you, brothers," he said when they finished.

They decided to leave him with a few biscuits, liquid milk, bread, and sardines.

"He reminds me of Sajid," Claudia said as they walked across the river.

"Really? Sajid is gorgeous," Hassan responded.

"Ha! What are you insinuating? That he isn't good-looking?" Kingsley asked.

Hassan said, "No! Come on! OK, wrong choice of words. Of course, he looks great. I'm just saying that Sajid looks be … OK, you know what? Forget it. There's no appropriate way to put this."

"Remind me again why you're discussing their looks," Bara asked.

"Please! It's not that deep," Claudia responded.

"I wonder what will become of him," Linda said as they stepped into another field.

Isa stood and stared up. "Not once in my life did I ever think I would be this satisfied from just seeing the sky."

"Or feel the wind blow against your skin," Bara responded.

"I never thought I could stay for days without taking a poop," Kingsley said, and everyone laughed.

The field narrowed into a footpath that went through a bush of elephant stalks and then meandered back into the jungle.

"Oh, God! Not again," Claudia cried as they stood at the foot of another hill.

Kingsley said, "Really? You're not even carrying anything. I'm so envious of girls right now. You always have it so easy."

"Easy? You have no idea what you're talking about," Linda said.

"But I do. We've all been taking turns carrying your bags and Claudia's bags," Kingsley replied.

"That's called being gentlemen," Claudia said playfully.

"Exactly my point. We have to be gentlemen even while in need of help ourselves," Kingsley responded.

"Kingsley, please, let's not get into this argument. Trust me—you'll lose," Linda said.

They embarked on another hill and their silence was constantly interrupted by strenuous groans as the hill became steeper and harder to climb. The exhaustion crept in slowly and effectively as the heat grew to unbearable temperatures. It became almost impossible to feel the difference between the air they inhaled and the air they exhaled. It was suffocating.

"Take it off! Take it off immediately!" Claudia yelled as they arrived the hilltop. She had found the heat unendurable, and her lugs had to go—it didn't matter how stunning they looked. She slumped down by a tree.

"Are you sure?" Bara asked.

"Cut it off! Please! The heat is killing me!" she insisted.

"But there isn't a razor, Claudia. How do you expect us to cut it?" Kingsley asked, fanning himself with a short branch.

"Use the machete. I don't care, just take it off. Quick please, I can't breathe!" she insisted.

Pastor was the only one who had not thrown anything away since the beginning of the journey. He held out his machete, and one by one, with Claudia holding the roots, he chopped off every one of her lugs. The temperatures did not change, but she did claim to feel better.

"And you still look good too," Bara said as they began descending the rocky hill, improvising every available style of motion, including walking, creeping and everything in between.

Halfway down the hill, they saw a body under a pile of tree branches on the footpath.

"God, please, I cannot handle the sight of another death in this jungle," Linda said.

"What must have happened?" Isa added a few more branches over the lifeless body.

"What a tragedy. Honestly, I don't know how much more I can take," Kingsley said.

"Let's just go please. The longer we look, the weaker I get," Bara said.

They proceeded down the eroded hill with spectacular jumps and daring maneuvers, and they emerged on another vast and scantily shrubbed field.

They walked for a mile or two and in a modest distance ahead, was a river that roared like none they'd heard before. Like a tiny figure, a woman stood in the middle of it with a backpack on her back and a toddler sitting precariously on her waist. The river flew violently down its course, its water level seemingly rising with every step she took. As if to measure its depth, she cautiously dipped a foot. The water pushed her, and she dangled but regained her balance. She took another careful step.

When the water reached the baby's buttocks, the river pushed her again.

"Oh my God!"

"What is she doing? Somebody, tell her to wait. Hey!"

She fumbled as she turned to the voices. As she tried to regain her balance, the water pushed the baby out of her hand.

"Mama! Mama!" the child cried as she struggled for a grip.

Isa dropped his bag and rushed into the water, but he was too late.

The woman screamed when she finally lost hold and saw her baby somersault downstream, toppling like a loose rock.

Isa dashed behind the little boy, and for a moment, it did appear like he knew what he was doing. Then he began tumbling too.

"Isa, are you OK?"

Isa tried to raise a hand, but he quickly toppled over again, clearly out of control.

"Dear God, that man is drowning! He's drowning!" they shouted.

Pastor started slowly into the water to help the woman. The rest ran downstream, screaming in pandemonium. The banks narrowed and ended as the river meandered into an impermeable section of the jungle. "Isa!" They screamed as they observed and saw nothing but the dim, breezy water coiling away into the dense woods.

Pastor managed to walk the woman out of the water.

"My baby! My baby!" she wailed in French.

Bara said, "What just happened? Are we in a dream? Isa was just … He was … I mean I …"

It truly did feel like a dream. So much had happened so fast, and it was impossible to take it all in. In minutes, two human beings had been swallowed by this reckless river that continued to flow carelessly before them.

Kingsley said, "So, we're not going to do anything? There must be something we can do! We should be doing something … and fast! We can't just stand here and whine like a bunch of babies!"

Pastor asked, "What do you want us to do? Do you think we don't want to jump right behind him? But of what good is that when none of us can swim?"

Claudia and Linda sat by the woman with their arms around her as they tried to comfort and console the woman through tears of their own. "Take heart, my sister. It's OK."

"No, it's not OK. My poor innocent child. What else am I living for? There's no reason to live. Not anymore. I lost his father today. He fell and hit his head on a rock while we were descending that hill. Now, what was my reason to keep living is also gone."

"What! That was your husband?"

At that point, all the statements of consolation—take heart, be strong, it'll be all right—sounded ridiculous and unreasonable.

They prayed with the woman and stayed by the river for almost an hour, watching in silent melancholy as it flowed, reminding them of their next challenge.

"Bara," Kingsley whispered as he moved toward his cousin.

"Yes," Bara answered.

"I'm bothered. I do not know a thing about swimming. How will we cross this river?" Kinsley asked. "If only I planned for this journey ... the war took me off guard."

"Tell me about it. One day, I'm in West Africa, and the next, I'm in South America. Not in Sao Paulo with Brazilian chicks like I've always dreamed or in a resort somewhere in Chile, but here in the jungle. Escaping anacondas and watching babies drown." Bara looked around in regret.

Kingsley said, "So, what are we going to do now? This river is clearly deep and fast. I honestly don't know where this woman found the courage to even attempt crossing it."

"You're going to have to find that courage, bro—unless you want to remain here, or return to the island, which will take you days of ascending and descending despicable hills and likely, another anaconda experience. And just so you know, it ran away last time because we were in a group. Alone, you're going to be one sweet meal. Did you see the movie *Anaconda*?"

"Bara, come on. Please stop. Not that I haven't thought about it, but going back is really not an option. Besides, we're no longer allowed on the island. Our permits expired, remember?"

"Exactly! Now you see why gathering the courage to cross this river is the only choice we have?" Bara said.

"But it's really not about courage. We can always brave up to cross the river, but how do we do it?"

"We'll find a way." Bara rose and walked over to Pastor.

"Did you hear that? Kingsley asked.

"I did. Pastor, can I speak with you for a moment?" Bara asked.

"I know. We need to leave now," Pastor said, returning from the spot where he'd excused himself to urinate.

It began thundering, and rainclouds were slowly obscuring the sun.

"We all know the water level will rise if it rains heavily. We had better be on the other side before it became even more diff— "

"I know, Bara. I'm trying to think," Pastor said.

"What's going on?" Hassan asked.

"We need to get on our way," Kingsley replied.

"I thought as much," Hassan replied.

They picked up their bags and walked through the thick, bushy banks toward the upper course in hopes of finding a shallower section, but that expedition proved futile.

Pastor cut a stick that was a little longer than his height and led the way in. They'd distributed the females evenly. Claudia was between Pastor and Bara, Linda was between Bara and Kingsley, and the poor grieving Haitian woman was between Kingsley and Hassan. Solomon trailed the group.

They held tightly to each other's hands, forming a chain, and they began shuffling sideways. Before every step, Pastor shoved the stick in the water to determine its depth. The stick sank pass its middle—and so did Pastor behind it.

Bara looked at Claudia, and his heart sunk. She was a stunning girl, but God had denied her height. And if it had ever been unfavorable to be short, it was now. "Are you OK?" Bara could only see her from her shoulders up.

Claudia nodded, and they proceeded behind Pastor. Inch by inch, the water rose until it was just beneath her neck—and her backpack was completely buried by it.

"Wow! Just great … perfect!" Kingsley muttered as it began drizzling.

In a hurry, they took in a few more steps. The far shore was seemingly out of reach.

"Faster, guys! Faster!" Pastor said as the thunder roared, and the rains descended heavily.

"Claudia, are you OK?" Bara asked.

The water was up to their chests, and it was up to Claudia's chin, frequently flying into her mouth. In a few steps, it became almost impossible to keep her nose above the water—or advance.

"Come on! Just a few more steps, and we'll pass the deepest part," Pastor called.

Courageously, Claudia aimed for another step, and the water covered her eyes. Claudia appeared to be struggling for air.

Without a thought, Bara let go of Linda's hand and lifted Claudia above the water.

"Bara! Jesus!" Hassan screamed. He held strongly to Linda, but the river was dangerously pushing back on her.

"Oh my God!" Bara panicked and accidentally let go of Claudia when he turned to help Linda. He staggered but managed to regain some stability.

The water swept Claudia away. Pastor gripped her with the strength of a virile man, but she floated away and screamed in agony as she hit her leg on a stone in the opaque water.

"Hold her! Hold her, bro. Please hold her!" Bara yelled. He got a hold of Linda after helping Kingsley pull her back. "You can do this, babe! You can do it. I swear, Claudia, I'll kill you if you let go. Please!"

"Jesus! Jesus! Jesus!" they screamed.

With one hand, Pastor pinned his heavy stick to the riverbed and dragged Claudia strenuously against the resistant water. As Claudia struggled toward him by means of rudimentary swimming techniques, she hit the stone again and found her footing. Pastor advanced carefully toward her and helped her balance on the stone.

Bara took a deep breath.

She stood up, although weak and almost paralyzed by fear, she was well above the water from her shoulders up.

With his stick, Pastor felt that some sand had accumulated by the stone. He maneuvered his way to the sediment, and when he stood, he noticed with infinite relief and gratitude that the sediment spread toward the banks. When he'd finally gotten a stronger hold of Claudia, he threw the stick to Bara, and he led the rest toward the stone.

With their hands held as tightly as before, they proceeded slowly and cautiously on the sediment that rose gently and then visibly entangled with the smooth pebbles that swept to the shores.

They staggered out onto shore. Their backpacks and bodies were dripping wet from the river and the rain that would not cease, but that didn't matter anymore. For all they cared, it could rain cats and dogs. They'd all made it to the other side, and thankfully, Claudia's injury had not been fatal.

CHAPTER 13

MAYBE THE STARS had come up, mesmerizing every eye with their dazzling colors. Or maybe a full moon had arrived, and as usual, showered the horizon with its glorious gold. Perhaps it was a beautiful night, but who knew? Certainly not Sema, Gilbert, and their two mates in captivity.

They'd sailed the ocean for days, and it was almost dark when they anchored and were led into the back of the military truck that sped to only the military and God knew where.

Sema was dying to ask Gilbert what he thought must have become of his pregnant wife, Solange. Not that it would change anything, but perhaps he just needed the assurance of a second opinion. With the stone-faced officer sitting by them, no one would dare make conversation. So, they sat aghast on the stationary bench in the dreadful silence that was worsened by the officer's fixation on them.

"Out!" he ordered, while standing.

None of them understood Spanish, but the officer's hand gestures were obvious. So, they followed him out and received immediate orders to walk straight into the room that stood a moderate distance ahead. Indeed, the moon had come up and shone defyingly in a fierce competition with the yard lamps, but so far, all they knew was they were in a gated establishment, heading toward a room out of which came indiscriminate voices.

In the room, a few officers appeared to be in a fun debate. The one at the table by the door waved a hand casually, signaling them to come forward. Then just like an old chore he'd grown weary of, he tossed an open book before them on the table and indicated that they fill in the blank spaces.

At the top of the page that carried uncountable names and signatures, there was a group of words in Spanish. Sema could hardly pronounce them, but it was jaw-dropping when he read that the English translation beneath ended with Panama City. At the next counter, another officer murdered their African names as he called them up from the bench and collected their fingerprints. The third officer approached and gave them a thorough body search. He found some money hidden in their socks and put it in plastic bags, which he labeled with their names.

They followed him down a corridor that was faced from both sides by rooms of prisoners. They kept shouting and banging on the bars as the migrants passed with their heads down and were locked up in the last room on the left.

Gilbert said, "Did you see what I saw? Sema, we're in a prison in Panama City."

"Don't you think I know that?" Sema asked as he paced the tiny room.

There was a bunk bed with a mattress that was intended for one person. Right by it, was a toilet that was surprisingly spotless. They stood on the rough cement floor, which was adequately lit by a white florescent bulb.

The prisoners in the next room began banging on the wall.

"What shall we do, bro? This seems like a very dangerous place," Gilbert said.

"Let me think, bro! Let me think!" Sema replied.

The two men with them from Nepal, had gone straight to sleep on the lower bunk, and even in their state of limbo, Sema and Gilbert knew that they needed to do same.

It would be risky for the two grown-ups to share the upper bunk. Gilbert decided to sleep on the floor since he was a bad sleeper. "It doesn't matter what position I sleep in, bro. I'll roll myself down—or I'll push you down that bed."

The morning might have come earlier than wanted for the prisoners, but the migrants had woken up even earlier.

One of the Nepali guys said, "I hope it works, bro. I really do. I once watched a YouTube video on Panama City's jail, and if it was this particular jail, we don't stand a chance at safety, if they send us out on the same yard with these prisoners."

"It has to work. That's the only plan I've got—so we can as well be positive about it. No thoughts of scary prison YouTube videos please," Sema said.

"Wait! I think they're going out now," Gilbert said as the doors clattered louder and closer.

The officer opened their door and said, "Time for breakfast." He spoke in Spanish while gesturing self-feeding. He waited to shut the door behind them, but when no one moved, he repeated, "It's time for breakfast!"

No one moved a muscle. In irritation, he banged the door, locked it, and then left. He might have believed the issue was the language barrier, but the migrants had just embarked on a hunger strike.

Hours passed, and the officer came back. He announced that it was yard time as he opened the door. No one moved, but that may have had more to do with fear of being mixed up with hardened criminals than it did with the strike.

Then it was lunchtime, then dinner, then a day and another, with different shifts of officers.

"I'm hungry. I don't know how long I can pull this off," Gilbert said. "We've been starving for two days, and no one cares. Bro, I'm sorry, but it seems like your strategy isn't working. We might as well just eat."

"What is wrong with you?" Sema asked.

"I'm tired, bro! We cannot keep doing this. It's not working," Gilbert insisted.

The Nepalese discussed for a while in their native language. Then one of them said, "Sorry, bro, but we agree with him. It was impossible to sleep last night with the hunger. I stayed wide-awake, and no matter how much I tried to avoid it, I still caught a glimpse of those scary prisoners across from our cell raising their middle fingers at us."

"So, what's your plan for getting us out of here? Are we just going to remain here and become prisoners? Until when? Do you think it's easy for me? I have a pregnant wife somewhere in the jungle," Sema replied. "Guys, please, it will be more effective if we do this together. Let's do this for one more day, and I promise they'll come for us, but if they don't, then you can go ahead and do whatever you want" he added.

It was breakfast time on the third day. Except for the migrants, everyone else had gone out as usual. An officer took a stroll down the empty corridors and found them in their cell. He looked new and more decorated than the others. "Who are you and what are you doing here while it's time to eat?" he demanded in English, after learning they didn't understand Spanish.

"We're migrants, sir. We've been locked up here for more than two days now. We have not been told for what reason or for how long we're intended to be kept. We shall not eat anything here or go out on the yard until our issue is addressed," Sema replied.

The intimidating officer scanned the frail migrants and then turned and left without uttering a word.

Sema exhaled and said, "That was scary!"

"We might have gotten ourselves into more trouble. Notice how he didn't say anything?" Gilbert said.

"I don't know. Let's just keep our fingers crossed," Sema replied.

A few moments later, an officer came by their cell and asked them out. It wasn't meal or yard time. So, not to be too hopeful, they concluded that perhaps the officer wanted to change their cell. They followed him to the room where they'd given their fingerprints.

Panamanian men were quite dashing, but they were a little below average height. So, it was threatening to see the huge man in the middle of the room talking authoritatively to the other officers. He turned and swiftly left the room.

There was an awkward moment of silence before the two officers in the room began whispering to each other. One of them beckoned the migrants to the table, and his colleague sat at the counter behind the computer, punching endlessly at its keyboard.

They signed again by their names, and after a few minutes of waiting, the officer at the counter called them out and handed them documents that permitted them two days in Panama City. He returned their money and asked them to follow him. In a thirty-minute ride, the officer would bring them to the bus terminal, and they were expected to find their way out of Panama.

They rushed to the nearest snack shack and ate and drank like beasts.

"I told you guys it was going to work," Sema said.

"Thanks for your persuasion, bro. Had we given up and gone to eat, perhaps the captain would not have met us—and who knows how long we'd have been in there" one of the Nepalese said.

"How do you know he's the captain?" Gilbert asked, finishing his third drink.

"He was more decorated than the rest. What else would I call him? I'm not familiar with military ranks and jargon."

"I see. Well, thank you too, bro. I was ready to quit. I'm not as strong as you are. I like my easygoing life," Gilbert said.

"I know. You're a spoiled thirty-year-old man-boy," Sema joked.

"And I have absolutely no issue with that," Gilbert said proudly as they laughed.

"Anyway, I would normally suggest that we retire to a hotel for a shower and some rest, but you know what? Let's just pay our tickets and leave," Sema said.

They finished their food and drinks and headed to the counter to ask for the town nearest to Costa Rica's border.

"What food can do! I feel rejuvenated! All I need now is a thorough shower," Gilbert said scratching his neck.

"You have no idea. My skin is burning," Sema responded as they settled down on their bus.

CHAPTER 14

A **CLOUD OF DUST** escaped to the air as the heavily loaded truck sped along the unpaved road. "Finally! We made it at last!" It was their first sight of civilization in days.

"Why are they just standing there?" Kamali asked.

"I hate it. Last time we saw them gathered, two people had been brutally murdered," Kofi said.

The Cubans stood by the road and looked like they were ready to run back into the jungle at any time. Another truck approached them from behind.

"What's happening?" Ali asked.

The Cubans peeked from behind the trees and then stepped out when it was safe to proceed. They sprinted toward the truck when its driver stopped and began sharing water.

Vera and Solange were doing their best to keep up. "Save some please!"

The Africans arrived and joined in the drinking. "Thank you, brother," they said endlessly. It seemed like he'd had more than one encounter with migrants. He knew they came down the road, and he often passed by to render humanitarian services to those he met.

A police vehicle advanced toward them, and they dashed back into the jungle. And in a direction, none of them knew, they ran in deeper and deeper. They wanted to get as far away from the police as possible.

Emilda said, "Oh, dear God! They must have arrested Solange and Vera!"

Solange decided to surrender with Vera. "I don't care. They can go ahead and do what they want to do. I don't care anymore. I give up."

They were placed in the back with the truck driver, and the officers sped down the dusty road to a destination they had no clue about.

• • • • • • • • ● ○○○○○○○○○ ○ ○

"How do we even know if what you're saying is true?" Kamali asked.

Ali replied, "You don't know—and I don't care. I've told you what I heard. Whether you believe me or not is up to you."

"Damn!" Kofi said.

Kamali and Kofi moved away behind the Cubans.

"You've always taken the high road, Ali. That's one of the reasons I chose you. Remain you," Emilda said.

"Nope! I'll give him a taste of his own medicine. Let him understand that it's not an inability; it's a choice to stay quiet through his childishness," Ali said.

No one knew for certain if Ali was telling the truth when he said the Cubans had explained that they weren't allowed into Panama's immigration camp and would be returned to the island if caught. Ali insisted—as he always did when anyone doubted him—that he'd taken Spanish in high school and had kept it up by watching telenovelas.

They wanted to return to the dusty road, but they were all lost. Their only choice was to stick with the majority. It was always a safer option. They followed a narrow path that wound up in a valley that harbored all breeds of mosquitoes and insects. Through the stinking spirogyra-infected stagnant water, they walked and then crawled out of the valley and found themselves in a section of the jungle that was like none other they'd been in.

It was depressingly shadowy and silent, and its trees were interconnected by creeping plants that were thorny. Movement was almost impossible. They stood still for a while, and the Cubans got into an argument about what to do next.

Emilda, Kamali, and Kofi did not understand a word that was being said, but Ali answered a few questions from the Cubans—even if all he mostly said was *sí*.

Well, some people are passively bilingual. Or maybe Kamali was right for once, Kofi thought.

To their immediate left, a footpath curled underneath the overlapping trees. As they followed it, they were constantly greeted by thorns and annoyed ants. The path gradually became fainter and fainter until it finally disappeared, bringing them even more hopelessness.

As they waited, they saw a sparkling blue river that neatly punctuated the jungle. It was not far from where they stood. Another footpath was marked clearly across the river. They began making their way through the thorny bushes to reach the footpath, but then they remembered that quiet rivers run deep.

A majority of the Cubans could have easily swam across if they mustered the strength, but it didn't feel right to leave others behind, especially since most were their women. Plus, there wasn't any certainty that the path would not stop abruptly into the jungle—like the ones they'd previously followed. They made a U-turn, but they got lost and wandered around in circles for hours.

The sun passed the horizon, and the sky was growing darker. Dusk crept in with nothing but an uncomfortable cold and more fear. The fear of passing the night in that deadly section of the jungle grew. There were robbers and the fiercest mosquitoes and insects.

They were perplexed and exhausted and considered giving up. The girls were crying, and the guys were out of ideas.

As if by divine involvement, they heard a horn. With excitement and hope, they leaped toward its direction, pushing and tearing their way through the woods.

One of the Cuban girls shrieked in agony and flung herself to the ground. She had accidentally shaken ants from a tree branch, and they did not spare her sweaty, tired flesh. She screamed and wriggled on the ground.

"Sorry. Sorry. It's OK," they said as they beat the ants off her skin.

"I'm tired. I don't care if they send me back. I don't care anymore!" the girl yelled at one of the guys who stood consoling her.

Kamali whispered, "He's definitely her boyfriend."

"Or her brother," Kofi replied.

"Nope! They don't look alike, and only a lover would take such arrogance," Kamali said.

"Wow! Then we all must really love you," Kofi replied.

"Whatever ... rubbish!" Kamali said.

"Listen."

Another horn sounded from the opposite direction.

"From which direction was that?"

"I couldn't tell."

One of the Cuban guys suggested that one of the Africans should help climb a tree to detect which direction the road was by checking for dust.

"No! Not happening," Kamali said. "Why only us? He looked at us and thought, oh, these Africans must have lived in trees—so they have experience climbing them. "You can go ahead and climb if you want. As far as I'm concerned, we might as well pass the night here."

"I agree with you on this one," Emilda said.

"Thank you! Great! For once!" Kamali said.

They stood in a circle, contemplating, and the Cubans probably believed that they were deciding on the climber.

"I agree too," Kofi said.

"Yeah!" said Ali.

"I mean, why would they automatically assume that we can climb trees?" Ali said.

"Exactly!" Kamali whispered.

Ali said, "But this is our safety we're talking about, guys! We've been going around in circles trying to find a road to get out of here. We've been in the jungle for days, but this is the most life-threatening section of it. I don't know about you guys, but I don't want to sleep here—and the night is fast approaching,"

"Of course!" Kamali responded sarcastically.

Ali decided he would climb the tree, but the truck had long passed by then. They waited for close to half an hour before another truck came by.

Ali sprung and climbed up the tree like a seasoned climber.

Kamali said, "Go ahead, bro! Enforce the stereotypes. Oh my God. This is so embarrassing! Look at him. They're probably saying he's like a monkey!"

"He would know if they were. He understands Spanish" Kofi responded.

"Please!" Kamali replied.

In a minute, Ali was down from the tree and revealing the direction of the clouds of dust.

They fervently followed his lead and finally came to a footpath that gradually widened as it cut through the banana farm and then descended to the main road.

With extreme relief and delight, they proceeded up the earth road.

A woman on her way down the hill directed them to the immigration building.

The Cubans divided into two groups of conflicting interests: those who would not risk a return to the Colombian island and those who were worn out and thought the immigration officers might have the compassion to help them with their journey.

Voices became louder and clearer as they approached the simple gray building on the hilltop.

"Here we are, finally" Kamali said.

Two police officers stepped out and ordered them inside. They collected their names, fingerprints, and nationalities. All the Cubans were called out to a police vehicle and taken away.

In a gated hall across the road, hundreds of migrants of all ages were eating, gossiping, laughing, and comforting crying babies.

They felt the weight of a thousand pairs of eyes fixed on them as they came in.

"Emilda!" someone called from the crowed.

"What!"

"You ended up here!"

"Thank God you're safe."

They hugged Solange and followed her past countless plastic mattresses, to the extreme end of the hall where she'd settled with Vera.

"Have you heard what happened?" Solange asked.

CHAPTER 15

THE SUN HAD come up brilliantly, slowly drying up the dew from the glistening wet leaves. With all its saga and tragedies, the past few days had been overwhelming, and they had benefitted from little or no sleep. In fact, a sound sleep was far-fetched, especially with the Haitian woman weeping nonstop.

That morning, they had met another span of stunning basaltic rocks on which they'd sat to eat their breakfast. The Haitian woman was still weeping in loud sniffs as she sat alone some meters away from everyone.

"I'm short of words at this point. I don't know what to tell her anymore," Kingsley said.

"Come on. You don't expect her to just stop grieving. The poor woman just lost her husband and child. We don't have any idea how painful it feels to lose a child," Hassan replied.

"Well, all I'm saying is that she needs all of her energy for the rest of the journey," Kingsley responded.

"The woman is allowed to mourn her family, Kingsley. Leave her alone," Pastor said.

"Thank you," Solomon said as he received a container of chocolates from Hassan.

"Is there a problem with your inhaler? Hope the water didn't damage it," Hassan said.

"No. Luckily, the cap was on, so the water did not find its way in," Solomon replied as he shook off every particle of dirt from his inhaler and settled on some bread and chocolates.

Claudia lay on a rock and rested her head on Bara's lap.

Bara was eating from a packet of biscuits.

"I can only imagine how scary that must have been for her," Hassan said.

"She was so close to slipping off," Pastor responded.

"Yeah, I almost lost her." Bara gazed at her precious face, which was blessed with refreshing melanin that sparkled in the radiant sun as she slumbered. *How is it possible that she is this gorgeous, delicate, and powerful all at once? A compassionate social butterfly who knows all about slang and fashion and commands attention wherever she goes? Her face is sculpted so precisely, and everything is in its place. Does she feel like I do? Or are we just friends with benefits, like she said? Does she feel out of her mind when she thinks about me? Does she think about me at all? I wonder if she feels like her heartbeat is synchronized with mine—just like I do. How could I have let you go? My world would have been altered for the worst if I lost you, Claudia.*

"I feel weird," Linda said. "I know she said she wanted to be alone, but it feels terrible to sit here eating while she's over there crying."

"I feel bad too, but sometimes people need their space," Hassan said.

"I don't know! I'm going to her." Linda went over to the woman. "Dear, you have to eat something." She placed a comforting hand on her back. For several minutes, the poor woman cried and sniffed even louder.

"Claudia, Claudia, Claudia," Bara whispered as he patted her soft arm.

Claudia began breathing heavily and twisting her face. "No!"

"Jesus! Are you OK?" Bara asked, when Claudia suddenly screamed and jumped up in a panic. She held her hand over her chest as if to keep her heart from bursting out.

"Are you OK?" Bara shifted over and wrapped his hand around her shoulder.

"I had a nightmare about the river again," she replied.

Claudia had not been herself since that ghastly incident. She ate less and talked even less. She always wallowed in thoughts. Even when she did appear to be in a sound sleep, she sometimes screamed.

"It's normal to get nightmares after a life-threatening incident. Unfortunately, you're going to keep getting them for some time, but you'll be OK in the long run," Pastor said as he handed Claudia a bottle of water.

"Thanks," she responded weakly as she took the water and picked up a bar of shortbread.

They all gathered around her, even the Haitian lady, and they felt genuine concern for Claudia's well-being.

When Claudia finished eating, Pastor said, "OK, guys, let's pack up and leave."

They started across the field and then went around a long hill via a footpath.

They'd been walking for hours through the blanketing jungle, but they were now encountering fewer hills.

"I need to use the bathroom," Bara said.

"My God, Bara, did you have to announce it? Now all I can think of is you trying to sort out your money and change the plastic when you're done," Kingsley said.

Everyone laughed.

Pastor and Bara were among the many who had hidden their money in a condom and put in their most private of places. And now that Bara was going to empty his bowels, Kingsley could not help but imagine what other transactions would have to take place from sorting out the plastic, changing it, and then hiding it again.

Linda said, "Ha! He just said he wanted to use the bathroom. How do you know exactly what he wants to use it for?"

"Trust me, he would not have announced it if he wanted to urinate. He would have stood by the side and just done it," Kingsley replied.

"Shut up, Kingsley," Bara said playfully.

"Don't worry about it, bro. It isn't you alone," Pastor said.

"No way! What! You too?" Kingsley said.

"What? Did you hear the stories back on the island? Bro, prevention is better than a cure," Pastor declared.

"It's a good thing he bought plastic gloves," Kingsley said as Bara left.

Hassan said, "It's funny how the biological system automatically adapts to changing situations and even locations. I've only been pissing for the past four days."

"I know! But we've also been eating nothing but biscuits and bread," Linda said.

"Yeah, and we burn all of it climbing those mountainous hills," Kingsley said.

When Bara returned, Hassan said, "What took you so long?"

"Well, like Kingsley said, I had to change the con—"

"Oh my God! Let's go please!" Kingsley said and they all laughed.

They walked for hours before taking on another hill. The sun had begun setting, and the vibrant golden rays that pierced fiercely through the branches was now lazy and struggling.

"This is frustrating, to say the least. What do we do now?" Kingsley asked.

They had descended the hill, only to meet two diverging footpaths that were both clearly passable. Plastic bottles and candy packages littered both.

After a brief deliberation, they chose the path to the left. It looked more used, but Linda insisted that she'd seen her mother, who had long since passed, in her dream the previous night. She'd stood before two paths, nodded with a smile, and pointed to the one on the right.

"You were simply hallucinating."

"It was just a dream."

"I don't believe in such things."

"She cried each time I stubbornly insisted on taking the left road. Please let's take the right path," Linda said.

"Does it really matter? The paths probably just merge ahead," Hassan said.

Bara said, "To be honest, I just don't believe in dreams. My best friend dreamed once that he bought himself a Jaguar for his twentieth birthday. He got all excited about it. Now, he's almost thirty, and he doesn't even own a bicycle."

They all laughed.

Kingsley said, "Yeah! I had a dream in high school that I was the best in a biology sequence, but I ended up failing woefully. I'm sorry about your mother, my dear, but most times, dreams tell the exact opposite of what will actually happen."

The majority prevailed, and they proceeded down the left path. They walked for close to an hour before meeting another river. The sandy riverbed could be seen clearly through the crystal waters.

Bara said, "Are you good, Claudia?"

"I'm trying to be," she responded.

"It's OK. It's a shallow stream. Look at the riverbed. It's visible all the way across. Plus, I've got you." Bara held her hand so tight it almost hurt.

"Thank you," Claudia said as she crossed slowly by Bara with her eyes closed. She said it felt like the waters would swallow her up.

They made it another mile before they saw a group of three indigenous men. They appeared casual and normal and carried backpacks.

"Amigos!" They spoke Spanish and smiled.

They thought it a good sign to have started meeting the locals. It meant they were closer to human settlement and would soon be out of the deadly jungle.

When they were close, the men suddenly stopped and surrounded them with guns they'd hidden in their waists. "Clothes! Give your clothes!"

Pastor said, "What! Are you out of your m— "

One of the men fired in the air and then placed the deadly cold metal on Pastor's forehead.

They reluctantly took off their clothes and were left with nothing but underwear and shoes.

"*Todos!*" They ordered the girls to the side and watched them with a sickening admiration.

When every piece was off, the men confiscated their clothes and bags, gave the migrants the backpacks they'd brought, and dashed away into the limitless jungle.

In silence, they picked out and put on the clothes and shoes they found in the bags.

There was no underwear, and the shoes and jeans were funny, oversized, stinky, and all male, but they had no choice.

Hassan had been lucky. Before leaving the island, he'd tied up his money in a small plastic bag and inserted it in his socks. While taking them off, he'd clutched the little plastic bag with his toes. The rest of his friends, except for Bara and Pastor, had been robbed of everything.

"I swear, I'll curse those men. They won't go free. I'll curse all of them," Kingsley said as they left.

The Haitian woman had also lost everything. She couldn't stop crying.

"We shall get through this. Just have faith," Claudia said.

"I cannot believe that your backsides finally saved your money," Kingsley said.

In normal circumstances, the statement would have inspired some laughter, but the moment was too poignant to be amusing.

"I cannot believe that I regret not using my own backside," Linda said.

Pastor burst into laughter, provoking the others to do same as they examined each other's outfits.

"God! You look funny, Linda!" Kingsley said.

"Why are we laughing? We just got robbed," Linda asked.

Kingsley replied, "I don't care anymore, Linda. After all, moodiness will not change anything. At this point, we might as well just laugh off the dilemmas of this stupid journey."

"I guess! At least they spared our lives and dignity," Claudia said.

"Look, my backside is a part of my body, bro, and if I can use it to hide my money from being stolen, so be it," Bara declared.

"How do you think you'll be getting your prostate examination eventually?" Pastor asked.

"I don't think I'll ever get one. In fact, I'll pray and fast that I never need to get any," Kingsley replied with a laugh.

"Ha! It's your health, bro. That's all it means. It doesn't have to mean anything else," Hassan said.

"You heard the stories back on the island, and I warned you all, but you insisted on hiding your money under your shoes."

"And they took away our shoes," Bara said.

"Yeah, we get it. You told us so," Claudia responded. "I'm sorry we ignored your dream and dragged you into this. Your mother wanted to save us. We would not have been in this mess if we had considered what you told us."

Linda said, "Life is a learning process for everyone. I do believe in some dreams. I think God speaks to us in different ways, and sometimes in order to give us pertinent information, he uses people we can easily believe, but we're often too shortsighted to really understand."

"I agree."

"Totally."

"Makes sense when you put it that way."

They walked for miles, and when the sun disappeared, the cold and quiet of the evening crept in.

They saw a house and a road that ran past it. It meant they had finally made it out of the Jungle—out of the Darien Gap.

"Yes!"

"Yes!"

"Finally!"

They continued for another hour. Truck after truck passed, and a few offered them water, but most just raised the thick red irritating dust and sped on. And even though their joy had been too great to care about the dust, it quickly diminished, especially when Solomon began choking from another asthma attack.

"What are we going to do? This cannot be happening. Come on, bro. Fight it!" Hassan said.

Pastor put Solomon on his shoulder and raced toward the house. Its lawn was coated in the reddish-brown dust.

Bara headed straight to the door as Pastor laid Solomon on the grass. He was worried about the reaction of the owner, but Solomon needed urgent help. His inhaler had been taken away in the bag by the depraved hooligans who had robbed them. "Help! Help!" He banged on the door.

A girl in her twenties opened the door lazily, and her red, bulgy eyes said it all. She had just woken up from a siesta.

"Hello!" Bara pointed at Solomon wheezing on the ground.

She ran back into the house and came out with a phone to her ear.

Solomon's friends surrounded him and fanned him with their T-shirts. The wheezing grew worse, and he appeared to be getting weaker by the second. His ribs squeezed abnormally as he struggled to gasp for air.

In a few minutes, a police vehicle arrived at top speed. They hurriedly moved him into the backseat, and one of the officers found an inhaler in the first aid kit and they drove away. Two of their colleagues remained with the rest of the group. Another truck arrived and took them to the refugee camp, which was a few hundred feet away.

CHAPTER 16

THE DARKNESS OF the night had not completely gone away—and neither had their sleep. It was annoying to stand half-awake in the gender-separated lines in the freezing cold for the roll call that took place before their dormitory every other morning and evening.

The police officers in the little Panama refugee camp had mastered the golden rule of leadership: be kind, clear, fair, and firm. They were loved and revered even as they stood before the grumbling crowd of migrants and asked firmly for silence.

Hassan had become enthralled by Hendry, the slim Congolese guy who spoke eight languages. "I must be like him," Hassan said.

Henry walked by the officer for translations when they began counting the males, females, and minors of every country and then matching the numbers with the data they'd printed out from their system.

"Hey! Good morning, bro. My name is Hassan. I'm from Sierra Leone."

"Oh, nice to meet you. I'm Hendry, Congolese."

"I know. There was a lot of admiration and whispers about you this morning. How did you get to speaking so many languages?" Hassan asked as they retired to their dormitory.

"Man!" Hendry said with a huge smile. "I already spoke Lingala and Swahili at home and French while at school. Then I learned English, Spanish, and Portuguese at a linguistic center back in my country."

"Wow! Impressive, bro," Hassan said.

"Yeah, I do find it easier to learn languages. I think it's my own gift-, know. I've always preferred letters to numbers. Even back in secondary school, I'd hated all my math teachers, but I couldn't wait for literature periods."

"Ha—the story of my life," Hassan responded with a chuckle.

While others proceeded to their beds, Hassan sat with Hendry on his mattress, a few feet from the door. "Why did you choose this position to sleep?"

"I liked it," Hendry replied. "Anyway, like I was saying, bro, guys made fun of me and two other friends when we dropped physics for literature. I would have dropped math too if it had not been compulsory. They called us weak and said literature was for girls."

"Ha! I've heard that too. Unfortunately, that's the notion back home. The desire to pursue the arts is received as an acknowledgment of academic weakness, a failure to one's family, and most baffling, a break of masculinity for boys," Hassan responded.

"Well, my classmates finally changed their minds when I started using the sweet persuasive words and the alluring charm of poetry to get any girl I wanted," Hendry said.

"I bet!" Hassan said with a laugh.

They talked and laughed and shared their experiences into the bright morning.

The mesmerizing sun looked like it had risen to stay. Specks of dust danced in the soft golden rays that flushed into the hall through the tiny windows and the doorless doorway.

"Good morning, Hassan," Claudia said as she came by.

"Good morning, sweetheart. How was the rest of your sleep?" Hassan asked.

"I had a nightmare again," Claudia replied, yawning non-stop.

"Well, at least you did not scream. That's the beginning of progress," Hassan said.

"Meet Hendry. Sure, you already saw him this morning. Bro, that's my crazy but compassionate friend, Claudia," he said.

"Hello! I hear you're quite the linguist," Claudia said.

"Ha! I try," Hendry replied with a chuckle. "So, what was your nightmare about?"

"It's a long story," Claudia replied.

"Oh! I'm all ears, my dear. Make yourself at ease and tell me what is keeping your enchanting face gloomy," Hendry said as he blushed.

"OK! I should have probably mentioned that she's taken," Hassan said as he got up and pulled Claudia away before Hendry could say another word.

Hendry said, "What? I'm just giving her a listening ear, trying to be a good listener. What can a man do?"

"What's wrong with you?" Claudia asked.

"Be careful. He's good at poetry," Hassan said.

"Aw! Wait, why should I be careful? I think it's romantic!"

"Exactly my point," Hassan replied as they stepped out of the dormitory.

They crossed the earth road and went to a restaurant. The immigration building was filled with the military men and women who had received them and taken their information upon their arrival the previous night.

Claudia said. "I wonder where they took Solomon and how he's doing. The attack seemed severe."

"It did, didn't it? Well, likely to the hospital. To be honest, a part of me had given up on him before the police showed up. Thank God for that lady who called," Hassan replied.

They went to the mini shop by the dormitory, which was beneath a mango tree.

The little earth road was an extension of the main one and ran down to the river. It served both the locals and the migrant community for everything from showers to laundry and transportation for the farmers. On their right, before they descended to the river, there was another restaurant. A number of movable toilets were stationed a reasonable distance away from it, facing a vast soccer field.

"Looks like I won't be taking my bath during our time here," Claudia said as they stood on the little cliff above the river and watched the natives sailing away in boats. The migrant men, women, and children did laundry and took baths carelessly in the open. In their defense, they wore their underwear.

"I guess it'll really take some time to feel comfortable in water again," Hassan responded.

"I'll be OK. I just don't have free goodies for him." Claudia pointed to a male officer who stood guard underneath a cypress tree.

The officers thought the migrants might try escaping if they were frustrated with the duration of processing time in the camp. They stood on alert around the clock.

Hassan laughed.

"I need to find a way to brush my mouth," Claudia said.

"Yeah, you need to," Hassan joked.

"What! Shut up, Hassan," Claudia joked back.

"Ha! To be honest, we all need to," Hassan said as he followed her.

Two long lines stood before the immigration building. A nongovernmental organization had arrived, and all the migrants were receiving a backpack with a toothbrush, toothpaste, a comb, a roll of toilet tissue, and a bottle of hand sanitizer.

A group of nurses conducted a vaccination program. A few feet from the injection table was a heap of clothes for anyone who needed them.

"Whatever happened to just dropping the damn vaccine into the mouth? Ugh! I hate syringes," Kamali said as they stood in line for their shots.

"Tell me about it," Kofi responded.

"Thank goodness! We can finally get rid of these oversized rags," Claudia said.

"Come on, they are not that bad!" Hassan responded.

"They're oversized. Anything oversized is bad, Hassan," Claudia replied.

It had been too cold, and they'd all been too sleepy for chitchat in the morning when they'd gotten up for the roll call. All they had wanted was to go back to sleep. Now, they hurriedly joined the lines and before the exercise was done, they'd made acquaintances with people from their country and elsewhere.

"Hello! How far along are you?" Claudia asked.

"Five months," Solange replied.

"Wow! You're a strong woman, my sister," Linda said.

"I know! How did you manage to climb those hills?" Claudia asked.

They returned to the dormitory with injections and backpacks full of beddings and clothes.

Vera still walked like her legs hated each other. But at least, She'd been getting medical help from the officers.

They bypassed a group of Congolese women carrying buckets of rice and spices they'd been provided by the officers. It was their day to cook for the rest of the camp, but it was going to take a long time for the food to be ready, and no one wanted to wait.

Bara and the guys went to the restaurant to buy breakfast for everyone.

"I took the boat. It was equally a horrific experience. The military shot indiscriminately upon our arrival," Solange explained.

"Really? They seem different to me," Linda said.

Solange said, "That's because we're already here. One of the officers explained to us that back at the border, they cannot tell the difference between a migrant and a drug dealer. So, they approach everyone like a potential drug dealer."

"Yeah, he said drugs flow nonstop into the country through that road," Emilda said.

"Oh, that's horrible!" Claudia responded.

Linda said, "That's messed up for real! Our generation is messed—"

"Wait a minute! My friend took that boat as well," Claudia said.

"Why isn't she here? Her name is Eva, and she has a little girl called Ella, around seven years old."

"Oh, dear. I'm afraid I haven't seen anyone here by that name. When did she leave the island?" Solange asked.

"She left the same day as me. That should be six days ago," Claudia replied.

"Well, have you seen the videos?" Emilda asked.

"What video is that?" Claudia replied as they sat on Solange's mattress.

"Well, there were two boats the day we left. Ours and another that followed behind. Unfortunately, the second boat capsized, and almost everyone on board died," Solange explained.

"What? Impossible! I need to see the videos. She had a little girl. Her seven-year-old daughter," Claudia said.

"Sorry, sweetheart," Vera said.

They followed Solange and Emilda to another bed. Three Pakistani boys had a phone, and they giggled as they watched a video.

Solange asked, and they played a video from a dozen that sat on the phone's gallery. In it, recovered human bodies were set down on the sandy shore. The blue ocean was washing against their colorful outfits. Military personnel were filming and examining the corpses.

"This is her!" Claudia shouted. "That's Ella!" She put a hand over her chest. "My God! My God, where are you?"

Slowly, the camera drifted across the line of corpses—children, women, and men snatched from the flower of their youth. "That's Ella!" Tears dripped down Claudia's cheeks.

Ella looked just as innocent as she'd been while alive. The cruelty of death will always be disgusting.

"Take heart, my dear," Emilda said.

"How ghastly for a seven-year-old," Claudia replied. "On an earthly day, Ella would be running around, manipulating her mother's phone, and asking for chocolates. Adorably doing just what wasn't expected of her, you know, just like every other kid. Now here she is, stiff, and by a woman who isn't even her mother."

"Bara!" Claudia called.

"What's wrong?"

"Why are you crying?" Bara asked.

"The boat capsized and killed Ella and her mother!" Claudia handed Bara the phone.

"What do you mean?" Kingsley asked.

"What! Little Ella from back at the—"

"Yes, Bara! They all died!" Claudia said.

"Unbelievable!" Pastor said as they watched the video, stunned by the number of children affected. "I lost my appetite."

"Horrible. I lost mine too."

They gave back the phone and returned to Solange's bed.

"Thank God for this NGO. I was about to beg Bara to buy me a toothbrush," Kingsley said as they rushed to brush their teeth.

Regardless of the discomfort, they decided to go down the river for their baths. After the baths, they would change into better outfits. They returned to Solange's bed and talked about the boat tragedy and their experiences in the jungle. They consoled Solange as she constantly worried about her husband's whereabouts.

Before the day ended, two large buses arrived. Everyone ran out to listen to the immigration officer calling out the numbers of those who had been permitted to leave. Even though groups of new migrants arrived daily, the buses had taken away more than half the population and would come back the next day, like every other, for the next set.

CHAPTER 17

TWO DAYS LATER, they left behind the sadly cosmopolitan Panama refugee camp.

On both sides of the road, lush greenery spanned out for miles, but it disappeared into the faraway structures that were faintly visible to the migrants as they skimmed across Panama. From a distance, they admired the glassy skyscrapers of Panama City, which glittered in the arriving dusk.

Late at night, they arrived in the peaceful town. A group of uniformed men brought them into a hall that was vacant except for some torn cardboard boxes in a corner.

They rushed over to the pile, and those who were fast enough grabbed and spread out the cardboards as mats. They weren't the most comfortable things to sleep on, but they were better than the hard floor, which the others slept on.

"Whatever happened to Solomon?" Bara said.

"Oh! Pastor and I saw one of the officers who rescued him that day. He said Solomon was doing OK and would be out of the hospital soon," Kingsley responded.

"Yeah, he said he had to stay a little longer for a few checkups," Pastor said.

With babies crying from discomfort and their mothers comforting them, most of the crowd of about fifty stayed up and talked for the better part of the night.

"Up! Up! Up!" an officer said.

Morning had come, beginning another day for the refugees. The little town was busier than it'd been the night before, and everyone appeared to be rushing somewhere.

A clean paved road ran across the town and was more significant than any of the migrants realized. The uniformed men ordered them into a long line as they counted back and forth. Still on the line, they proceeded toward the road.

"Oh God! How humiliating!"

"I hope they didn't capture my face."

"What an embarrassment!"

Most of them hid their faces behind their backpacks when they noticed dozens of onlookers filming as they crossed the road.

"Welcome to Costa Rica," said the policewoman who received them on the other side.

Kamali and Kingsley agreed that she looked part Indian.

The woman distributed numbered cards and instructed them through Hendry to wait on the veranda. They were checked for their biometrics in three offices at the rear of the building.

"This is taking forever!" Vera said as the scorching sun penetrated the veranda. Even though they were badly in need of water and could have bought it in any of the nearby shops, they weren't allowed to leave.

"My god, I'm being baked!" Claudia said, hand-fanning herself. "Just two cups of strawberry yogurt right now will do."

After several hours, the last fingerprint was taken—and the bus whisked them away.

A man in blue came out of a little building that appeared to be his office. He opened the gate, and the bus rolled in and cruised to a much larger building in the center of the vast yard.

In the building, dozens of migrants were on their phones, gathered in gossip groups, or passed out in bed. The voluminous hall was filled with bunk beds and chilled by two gigantic mobile fans that had everyone yelling when they spoke. In a control room, three immigration officers distributed towels, body lotions, bars of soap, hand sanitizer, and toilet tissue. In the kitchen, migrants were provided with food to cook and serve three times per day. The dining tables were reserved mainly for the kids. Other people would eat wherever they wanted to eat.

Not that anyone looked for it, but alcohol had been a huge no-no in the Panama camp, and there were even more rules here. Although the locals found a spot the gateman could not see to sell ice cream and yoghurt through the mesh fence, the migrants were not allowed to buy it. They depended on the three-square meals provided by the camp's authorities.

The migrants chose their beds mostly next to their friends.

"She seems better now," Linda said, referring to their Haitian friend. She'd met and gone off with her fellow country people when they'd arrived at the camp in Panama, and though clearly still in grief, she appeared to be in a better place.

After settling in, a few of them went to the bathrooms that were attached to the back of the building. There were six for females and four for males with caricatures of both genders.

Solange waited for one of the bathrooms with her towel wrapped around her chest as she brushed her teeth with one hand and held a bottle of shower gel in the other. The person inside had been using the room for almost twenty minutes, and the other five rooms reserved for females were all occupied and had people waiting for them impatiently.

"What is she washing for so long?" Solange grumbled as she waited.

A door creaked at the end of the male section. It was loud and irritating, but Solange paid it no attention.

A deep, pleasant voice called her name. She turned slowly, and her frown quickly turned into a broad smile of genuine gratitude and shock when her eyes beheld the man before her.

Solange screamed at the top of her lungs and then burst into tears of joy as she and Sema ran and caught each other in a warm hug that would have been tighter—had it not been for her cute belly that had bulged significantly in the past week.

"Thank God you are safe." Sema released her and quickly picked up his towel, which had fallen from his waist. It was a good thing he'd worn underwear. "It's OK, baby. We are here now," he said as he wiped off Solange's blissful tears.

It wasn't usual for African couples to call each other by pet names like honey, baby, sexy, or darling. That mostly ended after the bridal price payment, and even the few who continued to do so afterward stopped after the first child arrived. From then on, they only called each other by a reference to their child's name.

"He called her baby!" Gilbert was still single and happily mingled with any girl. He had exited the bathroom and watched the elated reunion in delight—just like everyone else at the scene.

"Gilbert! I'm so happy to see you," Solange said.

"Happy to see you too, my dear," Gilbert replied.

Solange was not going to hug him, but Sema held tightly to her hand just to make sure. He was ready to pull her back if she even attempted to. He wasn't about to let his wife hug another man in towel—let alone Gilbert. Although Gilbert was his best friend, he was also a philanderer.

"What happened to you?" Gilbert asked.

"Where do I start? What happened to you?" Solange replied. "OK, let me quickly take my shower, and then we can talk all about it." She handed her husband her toothbrush.

"What would you have done with it if I wasn't here?" Sema joked.

"I have no idea! Well, you're here now," Solange called as she entered the bathroom.

· · · · · · · · ● ○○○○○○○○ ○ ○

After the steaming sun slowly disappeared behind the hills, the premises were covered by a permanent evening shadow.

Sema and Gilbert talked about their unfortunate experience and how they'd been permitted to wait in the camp for a few days even after receiving their permits. They'd been informed that no one by the names they mentioned had passed through. Solange, Bara, and the rest talked about the hills they climbed, the corpses they saw, the lives they lost, and how perilously close Claudia had come to losing hers.

"I will forever be grateful to Pastor" Claudia said.

"And I'll make sure to remind you of that," Pastor joked.

"I'm so sorry to hear that. That must have been scary," Gilbert said.

"Thanks. It definitely was," Claudia replied. "If I had not been beaten on the head so much while growing up, I would have probably been taller. Who knows?"

That comment provoked some laughter.

"I suppose you were very stubborn then."

"Suppose?"

"I don't even doubt it."

"Actually, I was," Claudia said.

They returned to the hall as it got darker and hotter.

Hassan stayed outside with Hendry and talked about languages. The guys gathered around Bara's bed and argued endlessly about Manchester and Liverpool, and the girls gathered around Solange's and talked about the businesses they'd had back home, what they'd do with their hair the next day, clothes, nail polish, and guys.

"So, you and Bara! How long has it been going on?" Emilda asked.

"Dear, you have no idea," Claudia replied after a brief chuckle. "Well, he's been trying his best, you know. Shooting his shot. But, honestly though, he's a great guy. I know I keep telling him and everyone else that we're just FWBs, but I'm starting to, you know, feel like there's something there to explore," Claudia said with a blush.

"So, why don't you go for it? What's wrong?" Vera asked.

Everyone was all ears.

"Well, no pun intended obviously, but I envisioned my man differently ever since from secondary school. He was supposed to be famous, tall, dark-skinned, handsome, athletic, and madly successful of course. Bara is kind, caring, and will do anything to ensure that I'm OK. Just that—"

"He isn't famous or madly successful? What does he do?" Emilda said.

"Does it matter? We're both refugees now," Claudia replied. "Anyway, I'll definitely have to work on his fashion sense. He's so choked up. Ties and hats and suitcases. You needed to see him the very first day we met," she added, provoking laughter they didn't mean to be so loud.

"And you, how on this earth did you get two Ethiopian men fighting over you?" Linda asked.

"I know, right? And why did you choose Ali over Kamali?" Claudia said.

"Well, first, I didn't get them fighting—they decided to fight. It got even worse when I chose Ali" Emilda replied.

"Yeah, Kamali seems like the jealous and troublesome type," Solange said.

"You know, initially, I thought he was interested in me, but I quickly realized he was only using me to make you feel jealous," Vera said.

"Poor you."

"Yeah, how dare him? That's bad. Emotions are delicate," Linda said.

"Ali is everything I ever wanted in a guy. He's sexy out of this world, broad shoulders, thick juicy black lips, and muscular, which is quite rare for an East African man … no pun intended at all."

Everyone interrupted with thirsty hums and chuckles.

"He's educated too. I know he claims to understand Spanish, but he doesn't get translations right seven times out of ten—but he really is. Most importantly, he's slow tempered. I grew up with a violent father. God knows I cannot deal with a quick-tempered man."

"Amen to that!"

"God knows!"

"I feel you!"

"Ha! I won't even tolerate that. Hit me once, and I'm gone—and I will only return with a lawsuit."

"But Kamali isn't a bad guy though. He's actually quite generous with his money" Emilda said.

Linda responded, "What! Really? Please hook me up," Linda said, stirring laughter. "No. Let me tell you girls something. If a guy is generous, then there's some good in him—and you can always make it work."

"He talks too much. You'll get exhausted just listening to him" Emilda said.

"I don't care! Just hook me up. I can handle that" Linda replied.

The guys also decided to discuss the night away. They talked about soccer and the failed political systems in their various countries. Kingsley mentioned the Haitian girl he had his eyes on, but they had not really ventured much into women before they began falling asleep. So, one after another, they quietly excused themselves and slumbered off.

Three notorious kids were screaming and running about. They woke everyone up from their sweet morning sleep.

"I completely understand why some people would choose to not have kids," Claudia grumbled as they woke up.

In about an hour and a half, three immigration officers began calling out names and handing out permits that allowed the migrants a maximum of twenty-five days in Costa Rica.

The document was presented in Spanish and English.

"Your twenty-five days start today. You are allowed to leave the camp anytime from now on, but once you step out, you will no longer be allowed in," Hassan translated for the French speakers.

They went to town, and after receiving help from some gracious locals and friends they'd contacted through borrowed phones, they drank, ate, boarded a bus, and bade their farewell.

CHAPTER 18

THE RISING SUN cast a soft, rosy hue across the blue sky, but the severe-looking Nicaraguan officers could not have cared less. There was an uneasy silence as the migrants stood in their midst, and the German shepherds that paraded around the secluded immigration center.

After collecting their personal information and some payments, an immigration officer with another government official led them by foot to a terminal. They boarded a bus, which they all agreed had seen better days. Unexpectedly, it sped nonstop like a brand-new locomotive.

Nicaragua was a natural beauty, but there was also an eminent feeling of danger in the air that many acknowledged. Although, the presence of the sturdy-looking officer in the bus may have been part of the reason.

They made stops at roadside marketplaces, and the migrants ate from the local restaurants and used the public bathrooms. In a day and a half, they arrived at the sparsely inhabited Honduran border.

They walked hesitantly toward Honduras, and they were met by a gaggle of horsemen.

"Amigos!" they called as they galloped by.

The migrants could have used a different means, but the border roads were strangely void of public transportation, and the few cars that drove by did not stop when they had indicated their need for a ride. They accepted an offer from the men to be transported on horses to the Honduran immigration center.

They piled up on the muscular horses in groups of twos and threes and rode on the rough, stony footpath that creeped into the thick browning bushes. It was the first time on a horse for most of them, and it was neither as comfortable nor as fun as they once might have thought. The stirrups were only available for the owner, and the inexperienced passengers were glued to their riders and friends sitting in front of them. As they galloped along, the clothing the owners had arranged for them to sit on fell off, and they sat on the horses' rigid back muscles. It was quite a painful experience on their backsides.

They rode through the vast ghostly bushes for more than twenty minutes.

Well, they look innocent and harmless, Bara thought as he brushed away the paranoia that suddenly gripped his heart. He remembered the sweet lady at the airport, the jovial taxi driver in Ecuador, and the friendly indigenes who had stripped them off everything, including their modesty. *Nothing in this journey has been the way it seems. Every smile has been a ruse.*

The horsemen stopped and claimed that the road from that point on was no longer safe for their horses. The migrants had to continue on their own.

Good riddance, Bara thought.

They walked through the bushes for half an hour and acknowledged that the road really was in no shape for horses. It got slipperier and then intersected with a paved road, which they followed to a bustling town that seemed half populated by migrants.

The immigration center, in a block of creamy white buildings, was screaming for renovation. Hundreds of migrants were protesting before it. Vendors were selling truckloads of ice cream and lemonade. Newspapers and media outlets were carrying out interviews here and there. They were talking to anyone who cared to listen.

"We've been coming here for ten days now. The officers keep telling us to go back to our hotels and wait. They won't give us any reason—"

"There is either bribery or racism going on here. They've been attending only to a particular group of people and—"

"Hello! What's your name and where are you from?" a journalist asked.

"My name is Amayuru, and I'm from Sri Lanka. We've been here in the sun since morning. After an hour or two of service, the officers shut the door and have not opened it since!"

Countless interviews were going on, and it must have been an incredible advantage for the TV outlets with journalists who understood English. They took back a lot.

"Hello, amigos," someone called and touched Ali from behind.

"Hey! You made it here," Ali replied over the noisy crowd.

It was one of their Cuban friends from the jungle. They probably would have talked more, but the Cuban guy seemed to be in a hurry to go somewhere—perhaps to find his friends.

The migrants proceeded through the crowd, bumping and pushing their way toward the building.

The door opened, and a man in a uniform stepped out.

All the cameras turned to him.

"Spanish? Anyone?" he asked.

Hassan and Hendry raised their hands, but another migrant was called up. He stood by the officer and translated sentence after sentence.

"We are currently experiencing more work than we had prepared for. Our orders have been for you to go back to your hotels and wait." He gave the translator blank sheets of paper. "These papers will be distributed according to countries. You are expected to find yours and write down your name if you have not done so since you arrived here so that we can have an account of you. We do not welcome any form of disorderly conduct and will act against it accordingly."

The papers were shared, and the names were taken. Many of them had been around for weeks, and they grumbled that the same exercise had been done every day to no avail.

Before the officer went back inside, he read fifteen names from another paper and asked them to follow him.

"I was here before those guys!"

"Me too! Why are they leaving before us?"

"Discrimination!"

Rumors were that some people had found a link through the back door and had dipped a hand in the pocket to expedite their way. The allegations were unverified, but they now believed them to be true, especially when they saw the fifteen migrants go into the building and collect their passes.

The officer had explained that the fifteen migrants had been there before everyone else, but many had called him a liar and took matters into their own hands. They attempted to force their way in.

"Stop! Stop!" the officer yelled as he pushed against the door. He was helped by his colleagues, but neither strength nor numbers were on their side.

The frustrated migrants pushed relentlessly in an uproar.

Abruptly, clouds of irritating smoke darkened the entire premises—and then endless coughing and cries of suffocating children.

The patrol police had released tear gas, and pandemonium had broken loose outside. Chaos was everywhere as the migrants picked up their belongings and ran back to their hotels, tumbling and falling on slimy spills of ice scream and water.

A gentle calm descended with the night. The little town's nightlife was vibrant, but few migrants would be taking part in it. The chaos of the day had brought a general feeling of insecurity.

Bara and his friends had not found a hotel to rent, which was usually the case with newcomers. They rented rooms in an unfinished family property with rooms that lacked comfortable beds. The owner and his sons put plastic mattresses on the floor, collected their rent, and happily went on their way.

"Wow! I would love to own a hotel in this town. Constant returns ... perfect business," Pastor said as they slumped down on the mattresses.

"Yeah, the more we come—and the longer we stay—the better for them," Hassan responded.

"OK! I have to check." Kamali rushed into the unpainted bathroom.

"What's wrong with you?" Bara asked when he finally came out.

The galloping on the horses' backs had left Kamali with bruises, and he could hardly sit.

"Bro, that is literally the case for most of us."

They laughed as Kamali struggled to find a comfortable sleeping position.

• • • • • • • • ● ○○○○○○○○○○ ○

The golden streetlights brightened the dark morning. The migrants were heading to immigration. Talks the previous day had been that an NGO bus was going to come by early in the morning—and the officers would give passes to transport any migrants who were present.

The morning was made more serene by the distant barking of dogs as the migrants walked to the immigration building. They had hoped to be the first—or even the only ones there—but groups of other people were waiting impatiently. The overall population of those present was nothing compared to the multitude who weren't. Most had simply said that the talks were not based on any official information, and they weren't going to disturb their sleep for mere rumors, especially since there had been many such that never came true.

That day, favor smiled on the steadfast and the extraordinarily lucky, including Bara and his friends.

Two buses arrived after thirty minutes. The migrants fought their way in and scrambled for seats, and those who ended up with none refused to step down. They said they were going to stand until they reached the destination.

As they took off, an immigration officer sat next to the driver.

"What a haphazard system. We're probably leaving before people who came here ten days ago," Kingsley said.

"Yeah, that's because they chose sleep over leaving," Kamali replied. "They could have been here like everyone else to find out if the rumors were true. So, the system is not to blame—they are." He adjusted his position to deal with the pain that wouldn't let him sit normally.

"But why wasn't the information official?" Hassan asked.

"I don't care, bro! I'm in. Would you give up your seat for anyone of them?" Sema asked.

"I mean ..." Kingsley said.

Everyone laughed.

"Exactly! So why do you even care to know?" Kamali asked.

• • • • • • • • ● ○○○○○○○○ ○ ○

It was almost evening when they stopped in another town and were led to an establishment that took their biometrics and offered medical care to those who needed it.

They waited in the noisy hall, and the exercise seemed to be taking forever.

Bara and Claudia stepped out for some air, but Hassan and Pastor thought they just wanted some time alone.

Kamali followed them for his own personal reasons.

"Where are you going?" Bara asked as he passed them by the door.

"For medical check, bro!" Kamali replied.

"But you're not sick," Bara said.

"Man! I need something for these bruises," Kamali whispered.

Claudia heard, and they all burst out in laughter.

Bara said, "Bro! We have bruises too, and I'm sure they'll heal in a few days. Come on, give it a few more days, man!"

"A few more days? You have no idea about the heat I'm going through down there," Kamali said, laughing.

"So what? You're just going to let a doctor see your bottom? What if it's a female doctor?" Bara asked.

"Bottom! Is that what we're calling it now? Well, would you rather it was a male doctor?" Kamali asked.

"Let the poor guy go check himself, Bara. It's a vital part." Claudia was unable to suppress her own laughter.

Kamali said, "I don't see why Bara is laughing. Kingsley said you hid money in your own bottom!"

"In my privacy, bro! No one had to see my backyard!" Bara replied.

"Look, all I know is that I'm in serious pain. If I don't get some sort of medication for these wounds, I may have to stand for the rest of the journey—and I'm not ready for that," Kamali said, which left them all in laughter.

The two chauffeurs stood by the roadside, chatting and puffing cigarettes. It had taken endless hours, but the migrants were finally returning with new permits with their faces displayed on the top right-hand corner.

Kamali had applied a medical rub and returned with the rest of it. He'd warned Bara not to even think about begging for it.

"I support you! Don't let him have it," Claudia said as they boarded the bus.

CHAPTER 19

A **LITTLE PAPER WITH** a number, a slice of bread, a bottle of Coca-Cola, and a disposable plate of rice and chicken were being distributed to the migrants as they waited for immigration in Guatemala City.

It had been another day's journey with two officers, appointed from the group that had gotten them arrested at the border. Guatemala City was unbelievably busy.

A man and a woman in their thirties cruised by in a sparkling yellow Lamborghini as the migrants ate jovially by the street. They drove back after a few minutes and parked a few feet away. With huge smiles, they greeted the migrants cheerfully.

The lady opened the back seat, which was filled with bread and pallets of soft drinks. They started with the kids, proceeded to the mothers, and then shared the gifts with everyone else.

"Thank you."

"Thank you so much."

"How kind of you. God bless."

The couple got back into their car, waved, and drove away.

Kingsley said, "I used to think that the richer people got, the poorer they became, you know? I thought money made them proud and arrogant—and sometimes even cold to the suffering of others. This couple challenged that perception. You could tell they wanted to give as they did so happily."

Hassan responded, "I believe the opposite. Not the part about the couple of course—I think they were sincerely kind—but I believe that generally the poorer people get, the worse they become. Poverty makes people angry and envious, and those two vices combined in a person, believe me, are more dangerous than the coldness of the rich."

"That's insane!" Kingsley protested.

"Next! Number forty-two!" Hendry called from inside, where he'd been taken for translation.

Kingsley said, "Rich people suppress the poor to remain poor because only then will they be seen and treated as rich. Their financial power allows them to influence politicians in power for their own benefit, which is usually to the detriment of the poor. So, the anger of the poor, my dear brother, is very well justified."

Hassan said, "I differ. People are poor because of their own bad choices. While the rich are out working endlessly and reinvesting their money, the poor sit in beer parlors drinking bottle after bottle while criticizing the rich. They go to church on Sunday and listen happily as their pastors tell them that it'll be more difficult for the rich to enter heaven than for an elephant to pass through the eye of a needle. And that promise of salvation that is somehow premised on poverty makes them comfortable in their situation, but you cannot blame the rich for the inability of the poor to make logical analyses beyond the parameters of what they are told."

"OK! Bara, help me out here. Hassan definitely lost his mind," Kingsley declared.

"Sorry, bro. I'm actually on his side," Bara said.

"Thank you, Bara! Claudia, do you agree with me?" Hassan asked.

"Nope! I agree with Kingsley. You guys are cruel," Claudia said.

"They definitely are," Ali said.

"I think they are just factual. I agree with them," Kamali said.

"Of course, you do!" Emilda said.

"I also agree with Hassan," Pastor said.

"What! We will no longer call you Pastor. You've been stripped of that title from now on," Kinsley declared.

They all laughed as they ate in the warm evening sun.

"Number fifty-nine!" Hendry called from inside.

"What a strange pastor," Bara said in laughter as he left for Hendry's call.

• • • • • • • • ● ○○○○○○○○ ○ ○

Darkness fell with its chill. The Guatemalan city was not a late city at all. It was barely eight o'clock, and everyone had locked up their restaurants and coffee shops.

The migrants arrived in taxis, boarded a bus, and sped away through the nearly empty streets that were littered with stray dogs. They slept through the quiet hours of the journey. In the morning, the driver dropped them off at a little border town. They'd been given a twenty-six-hour stay in Guatemala that would expire soon. They walked toward the Mexican border and surrendered themselves to the border police.

• • • • • • • • • ● ○○○○○○○ ○ ○ ○ ○

Women sat beneath a mango tree as their kids played obliviously around them. Younger boys and girls stood in pairs all over the spacious yard, chitchatting in the scorching heat and being observed by the officers on duty. A heavy gate led into the Tapachula immigration and asylum camp.

When they stepped down from the public bus, all they could see were solid structures with thick, windowless walls.

The official information was that the camp was full and would not take in any persons for a week, but some also said that late at night, on any days they pleased, the officials would open the gate and admit those who were around at the time.

They would sleep on the cemented yard for a week, but that was partly because they had gone to town and found that the hotels were filled up. However, throughout the nights they spent before the immigration, the gate had not been opened except for buses filled with Central Americans on deportation arriving at the camp from the United States or already processed and leaving it to their various countries.

Every morning, the officers distributed numbers to the migrants. Some would remain beneath the mango tree, eating the juicy fruit that was constantly pushed down by the wind, but the majority would go to restaurants for a good plate of fried plantains and chicken. From time to time, they might pay the owners for a shower and a bathroom.

"God, how much I need a phone! I miss Instagram!" Claudia said.

"How much I need you, Claudia," Bara said.

A gazillion stars filled the black sky, twinkling on a spectacular night. Bara and Claudia stood behind an old Land Rover jeep behind a restaurant. Soft, gentle music exuding through the cracked wooden walls.

"How much I do," Bara continued. "I go to sleep, and every night, my dreams are filled with images of you. Sometimes I wake up in the middle of the night just to see you breathing."

"You do?" Claudia asked. She'd always thought he was a heavy sleeper.

"Yes, I do. It's like madness. My every though and heartbeat carries a reminder of you. I love you, Claudia. Come on, look at me." He looked straight into her enchanting eyes.

"I am looking," Claudia mumbled with just a hint of shyness.

"No. look into my eyes." He took her soft hands into his. "I am a simple man, Claudia. I can't buy you much, perhaps not even this crappy car … at least, not now."

Claudia chuckled.

"But I have love—true and genuine love for you—and I want to be more than just friends with benefits. We could go on coffee dates and dinner dates … at least that I can afford."

She giggled again.

"We could start from there, you know? We can do the small things, and we can do them together, if you just say yes and stay with me."

"What do you mean?" Claudia asked.

Bara stood silent for a moment. It wasn't hard to let out the words, but the possibility of Claudia's refusal was hard to consider. "I don't want to go to America. I want to remain here."

"Really?" she asked.

"Yeah! I mean, not here in Tapachula. Hassan and I spoke to one of the officers yesterday. He said it was possible to seek asylum here. All I have to do is indicate my interest to any of the officers when we get into the camp. I'll fill up some documents and answer to one or two interviews. I might still get denied, don't get me wrong, but I'm willing to at least try."

"Wow! I didn't realize you were serious when you'd mentioned it before. This is so much to take in. Why don't you want to go to America?"

"Well, the officer made us know that we'll be locked up for months, or even more, upon our arrival in America. Yeah, I'm definitely not going through that again. Plus, I can stay here. I'd asked in the previous countries, but the process was almost impossible. It's easier here. Come on! Apply with me!"

Claudia said, "I'm sorry. I can't give you a definite answer for now. I will have to think about it."

"We can go to Mexico City. I saved some money back home. We could rent a place and start a new life. It'll be difficult for a start, just like it'd have been in America, but I can finally learn to speak Spanish and pick up a teaching or translation job while you learn to design fashion like you've always wanted to. I'll support you all the way." Bara wrapped his hands around her waist and pulled her closer. "Come on—what do you say?" His manly hands rubbed up and down her back, and his moist lips were close to her forehead.

Claudia felt a warmth she could not deny. It was something; she would love. A genuine part of her wanted to grow used to it. Bara's heart raced in her ear as he held her even tighter. Her entire body was pressed against his. Her head was over his broad chest, but she could not tell if it was fat or muscle.

He tilted her neck and kissed her forehead.

A string of confusing but ecstatic emotions rushed through her heart, electrocuting her with excitement as he kissed his way down to the top of her nose. *Damn you, Bara*, she thought. The old her would have resisted, especially when it felt this way. She'd turned down men from every caliber and class: policemen, bankers, lecturers, and doctors. All she ever wanted was a hot Nollywood actor or an international soccer star. She had been told by the policeman that her standards were too high. Of course, they were high! Why would they be low? She'd said to him and a host of others who were way richer, more fashionable, and sexier than Bara. She could not understand why she felt this way about this man and why she felt happy to lead him on. *Damn my heart.*

Bara's lips locked on hers and kissed her deep like he had not done before.

She melted into his arms, and as if accompanied by the soothing rhythm of the music, they both left earth and went to another realm, where it felt like time stopped and waited patiently on them.

"Bara! Where is this guy? Big bro!" Kingsley called outside the restaurant, bringing them back to where they truly were: behind a dumpy jeep on planet earth—where time was cruel and thoughtless.

"God! He's annoying sometimes," Bara said.

They laughed and went back to the restaurant.

CHAPTER 20

ENTERING THE CAMP meant obtaining a permit to travel out of Tapachula, but it was still pathetic to see human beings eager and practically begging to be locked up—even if it was only so they could continue with their journeys.

In the chilly morning, they stretched out in long lines that extended from the gate to the yard. Migrants from Pakistan, India, Ghana, Cameroon, Congo, Haiti, Ethiopia, Nepal, Eritrea, and others represented the sad statistics of the world's migration crises.

It was said, that there were so many Cubans that they had an entire camp in town that was designated to them.

The officers counted and recounted. When the gate was opened, they proceeded in line after line until they were all seated under canopies for further evaluation.

The camp was nothing like they'd had in mind. It was a mighty establishment with another vast yard on the inside. In a semicircle around the yard, large and small buildings were sectioned by function.

They were each given a form that was printed out in Spanish, English, and French. After filling out the form, they would be separated according to gender. All the children, including the males, went with their mothers.

As they all got up to depart Bara, whispered, "Claudia, my intentions are not to put you under any sort of pressure. I would love for you to be happy—even if it hurts. Just think like you promised to and then follow your heart, OK?" He gave her a passionate hug that left her sadder and badly in need of more, especially when she saw him disappear into the room with the other men.

Linda said, "What he's asking of you is so selfish. Why can't he also follow you to America?"

"Well, he did admit that it'll hurt, but that he'll be OK if I choose not to stay because of my own happiness," Claudia explained.

"Aw!" Vera said.

"All he wants is my happiness. I'm so confused!" Claudia confessed.

"Over what?" Solange asked. "Look, my dear, any man who wants your happiness—even without him in it—is exactly the type of man you should go for."

Emilda said, "I agree. That was exactly how I knew Kamali was not the one for me. He knew I was happy with Ali, but he didn't stop coming after me and doing everything to ruin what we had going on."

Linda said, "If I were a man, I'd be so confused. I thought women enjoyed it when men continued to pursue them. So, why are we praising a man who just gives up?"

Solange said, "Not really. If a man keeps coming after you even when you've made it clear that you're happy with another man, then he's doing so from a place of control. He's implying that you're either happy with him—or you're not happy at all."

Emilda said, "Exactly! That is selfish, and that is exactly the type of man to avoid because if he is only happy about your happiness if it is with him, then it is really not about your happiness. It's about his happiness!"

"Well, if you insist!" Linda replied.

Vera said, "But you'll have to learn a whole new language. Do you really want the stress of that, my dear?"

They settled down with the others in the rowdy, jam-packed room and told Claudia what they thought about Bara.

Just like the girls, the guys were getting their backpacks and their contents labeled and registered. They were each given a card with a number to identify their property on the day of their release.

They proceeded through the bright corridors, which became noisier with every step forward. They came into another modest-sized hall with a glass control room. Two officers were watching soccer on TV. A few of their colleagues paraded in and out of the hall, holding their rubber batons.

They proceeded toward the door, bypassing a few other migrants who were talking with an officer in the hall. When they stepped out, they were astounded. They saw hundreds of men. Some were sleeping on green blankets on the cemented veranda, and others were sitting on the stairs that descended to a yard the size of two basketball courts. The rest were playing soccer or talking. It was hard to notice their arrival. They all dispersed to find others who looked like them.

"How many people are here, bro?" Kamali asked one of the African brothers.

"An officer told us that there are about five hundred," he replied.

"Wow!"

"I was not expecting there to be so many. Where do they all sleep?"

They sat together on the stairs, which overlooked the yard. It was dotted with security men, and a high stone wall divided the camp into male and female sections.

It was clear that 90 percent of the population were Central Americans, but the camp was an interesting composite of people from all works of life and diverse characters and beliefs. There were Christians, Muslims, Hindus, Buddhists and many who did not care about anything.

Pastor, Ali, and Gilbert watched the soccer match, and Kingsley and Hassan went to get a drink from the taps.

"Why is he going in there with that?" Kingsley asked as a man took an apple into the toilet.

"I know—nasty!" Hassan responded.

A loudspeaker announced that it was lunchtime, and the officers by the door called in the Central Americans. They rushed to the door and got in line. It didn't take long before they filled the entire dining hall, and everyone else had to wait until they had finished eating, which someone told the newcomers could take half an hour.

For the old migrants, whose stomachs were already singing to them, half an hour felt like forever. When they were finally finished and came out with their oranges, the officers called in the Asians and then the Africans.

The new migrants soon realized why the eating exercise dragged on for so long. Each person was required to find and sign their name on a list for attendance and then proceed to the long line to the kitchen, which was shaded by plywood. An opening at the base was just large enough for a plate, a piece of fruit, and a cup of water to pass through. Unfortunately, all the fruit was finished before the Africans arrived.

"Honduras! Nicaragua! Guatemala!" the loudspeaker called. The deportation buses had arrived, and the respective nationals were rushing into the hall. An officer was reading the names of those they had chosen to continue on their journey.

It was obvious when they had finished eating that the population had been reduced. Ali, Sema, Gilbert, and Pastor joined a few Central Americans to form a soccer team, but they had to wait until one of the teams on the court was defeated.

Hassan and Hendry had made friends with the Central Americans and were now speaking Spanish nonstop.

Kingsley and Bara went off to their own corner, and Bara talked about his plans with Claudia.

Kingsley wished them the best, but he said for the millionth time that he wasn't going to remain in Mexico. "I'll have to learn a whole new language."

"That is a good thing! You'll get it in less than no time," Bara said.

Kingsley replied, "Really! How many weeks have we been in South America, and all I can say, is *hola* and *pollo*? The only reason I know these two is because I need them to order food in restaurants."

Bara suppressed a laugh. "It's been a little over a month, but that's progress! Some time ago, all you knew was hola, and now you've added pollo!"

"Bara, please stop. Languages are not for me. I already speak our native language and English. Those two are enough. I'm a man of numbers, bro! Equations and formulas," Kingsley declared.

They talked and played and argued the rest of the day away. The somewhat sunless day turned even gloomier when evening arrived. In the same order as for lunch, they processed in for dinner. Once more, the fruits were gone when the Africans arrived.

The door that led to the yard was locked. They hurried through the corridors, bypassing numberless rooms, but all the bunk beds were already filled by those who had eaten first.

They scrambled for the mattresses in the corridors, and then they went to the general shower house, which was equipped with dozens of running showers. They stayed in the corridors since the rooms were locked.

The night-duty officers walked on a mesh ceiling and supervised all night long. Contact with the migrants at night was only permitted under exigent circumstances for their own safety, the officers claimed.

• • • • • • • • ●○○○○○○○○ ○ ○

One could always tell the arrival of daytime, even in a windowless detention. The migrants were up, and while the corridor sleepers were rushing for their morning baths, the Central Americans remained in their rooms until everyone else had freshened up and proceeded to the hall for roll call.

Two officers took turns reading the names. Each person was required to make certain that their name was checked before stepping out into the yard, which was already bustling with new migrants. There had been an intake that morning, and the newcomers had gone straight to the yard. When everyone was finally out, it was so loud that it was almost impossible to hear the next person.

"Excuse me!"

"I'm sorry."

"Excuse me!"

They pushed and squeezed their way through the crowd.

"Hey, bro!"

"Hello, bros! Good morning?" Sema said.

"Who are those guys—and why do they always greet you?" Kofi asked.

Sema said, "Oh, those are the two friends from Nepal I told you guys about. We were locked up together in Pan—"

"Oh, yeah! I remember," Kofi said.

"Yeah, they had left us in Costa Rica and tagged with their countrymen when we decided to wait on Solange."

"Understandably," Kofi responded.

They settled down by a short wall.

A gay couple sat on the stairs, minding their business. Their arms were entangled and one's head was on the other's shoulder. Then from the shoulder, he leaned down and slept on his man's lap. With their affectionate play and their constant tittering and giggling, it was apparent that they were in love. It might have been daring for the others, especially the Africans, but the Central Americans and Asians paid minimal attention to the couple.

"I hate these people," Bara said.

"You have no idea! If only I had a machete right now," Kingsley responded.

"They are lucky we're here. We would have beaten the hell out of them," Ali added.

"That's exactly where they're going—hell," Bara declared.

"I feel like choking them to death. In fact, let me leave. I just might do it," Pastor said as he went with Ali to the soccer field.

They stopped halfway, and Ali spat in disgust as the slender sylphlike boy passed them. He appeared to be in his early twenties, and the way he walked, the way he stood, and even his hand gestures when he spoke to his Latino brothers seemed to be queer and flamboyant in every way. His brothers would laugh at him from time to time, but they did not seem to care that he was different.

"That's another one," Kingsley said, pointing to the field.

"Have you guys seen this rubbish?" Kamali yelled as he returned from the toilet with Gilbert and Sema.

"My brother! What has society turned into!"

"It is spoiled. The world is spoiled. Look at this dirtiness!" Bara replied.

Hassan had been quiet all along, neither laughing nor contributing to their derogation and ridicule. He thought they were unsolicited, ignorant, and groundless. "Wow! So, on what basis do you guys pass all these judgments? What makes you think of yourselves as clean and morally validated to refer to someone as disgusting dirt?" he asked.

"Our culture! The Bible. Our religion! What are you trying to defend, Hassan?" Bara yelled.

"Their humanity! Their right to be exactly who they are!" Hassan yelled back.

"Get out of this place, man! Don't sit here and try to defend rubbish," Bara ordered.

Hassan replied, "Bara, no one judged you for fornicating with Claudia and the other women you've been having premarital sex with. You equally possess no validation whatsoever to pass judgment on these men. Worry about your own salvation. And for your information, you do not own this place. Just like you, I have the right to stand here if I want to. If you have a problem with me, then you be the one to leave. I am not going anywhere."

The queer guy noticed that Pastor and Ali and a few other migrants were staring at him and laughing. He turned, and even though it was obvious in his eyes that he'd known grave psychological torture, he appeared to smile—a weary, painful, false smile—and then he walked away.

The dining hall line started in the usual order. And when it was over, a few Africans were grumbling. There was another shortage of fruit. They brought out their tortillas and traded them to Central Americans. It was hard for them to believe that anyone did not enjoy their tasty tortillas. It was strange for them.

There was a tension between Hassan and his friends for the rest of the day. They couldn't agree that they had disagreed on such a matter. They pretended, but they knew for sure that Bara was extra pissed because Hassan had used him personally to make a point.

Hassan did not care. He and Hendry would meet to discuss poetry and politics. Hassan was called up by the administration for translation purposes, and he spent the rest of the day talking with other migrants. He even bragged to Hendry about the Hindi words he'd learned. The language was enticing for him.

CHAPTER 21

THEY HAD SPENT five days in the Mexican detention center. It was the same rowdiness and routine: shower in the morning, roll call in the jam-packed hall, yard, meals and a fight for mattresses in the evening. A lot went on while in the yard—constant arguments, soccer, and watching Muslims come together from different parts of Africa and Asia to pray—but many had begun to feel trapped in those revolving activities.

Everyone had moved closer to watch the new game. It was a game of coins, and the players were expected to throw a coin at a line from a particular distance. The one whose coin came closest to the line took everyone else's coin for that round. If two coins fell on the line, the round had to be repeated. The yields were not of any great significance, but it was fun to watch or play, and it helped kill the seemingly stagnant time.

Bara would rather not play. He sat on the veranda thinking about Claudia. He wanted so badly to know if she was on board with his proposal. *What if she says no? What if she chooses America over me?* Bara quickly discarded the thought. He could not live without her, and he wasn't sure he wanted to.

The previous evening, when the Africans had been the only ones in the yard waiting on their turn to eat, it had been relatively quiet. He'd heard her singing with the other girls on the other side of the wall. He'd missed her even more, and he had tried to convince Pastor that the camps in Panama and Costa Rica were better because everyone was kept together.

The crowd suddenly burst into a tremendous cheer and laughter. Kamali had won five straight rounds, and a few of his competitors had refused to continue playing.

Kingsley wanted desperately to stay in the game, but he had run out of coins. With one potential donor in mind, he scanned the busy yard and started toward where Hassan sat with the gay couple on the field. He stopped, a reasonable distance from them. *I don't want to get close to that nonsense,* he thought. Then he called for Hassan, and said, "What are you doing with these people? Stop disgracing us, bro. Look, people are going to start thinking that you're that way too. Anyway, lend me a few coins please. I'll refund them when we get out."

Hassan replied, "Don't worry. I'm not going to bring the sickness back to you guys. Take it." He handed Kingsley a few coins out of his pocket. "Not that I expect to get it back. You've not refunded any money you took from me."

"I will, bro. Come on. Why are you my brother if I can't stay a little longer with your money?" Kingsley quickly took the money and hurried back to the arena.

"Is he your brother?" Ortega asked as Hassan sat back down.

"Not really. He's a friend," Hassan replied.

Gustavo said, "Oh! You look quite alike. I'm sure he hates us, especially that you're sitting here with us."

"Well, yeah, he does. They all do but forget about them. It's just ignorance. Come on. Continue with the story, please." Hassan smiled sadly.

"Oh, OK. Well, when we received the fifth threat—through a letter slid underneath our door with sprinkles of a red liquid on the paper, which we guessed signified blood—we knew it was time to leave."

"Yeah," Ortega said.

Gustavo said, "So, we packed that night and left Nicaragua the very next morning. Our plan is to seek asylum here in Mexico. It's not 100 percent safe for us though."

Ortega said, "No place is."

Gustavo said, "But it's better than back in Nicaragua. The police laughed and called us the F-word when we reported the first threat."

Hassan replied, "I understand completely. I'm so sorry. It's cruel that the world is so lacking in empathy."

Gustavo said, "Thank you—a lot. You don't have to apologize. It was not by any fault of yours. They do not address the corrupt government for all the unemployment, embezzlement and insecurity forcing them out of their homes, but they threatened us for loving each other. Something we don't chose to be." He smiled.

"I know!" Hassan replied.

Gustavo said, "Anyway, let's change topics please. Something lighter. Let's start with you and where you learned to speak Spanish so well!"

"I try! You should meet my friend Hendry. He's way better than I am."

Kingsley yelled to Hassan from where he stood on the stairs with an officer and gestured for him to come over.

"Sorry, guys. I have to leave. Thanks for sharing your experience with me."

"No. Thanks a lot for your concern."

"Yeah, we really appreciate it."

"Anytime, bro. See you guys later." Hassan hurried over to the stairs.

They were heading to the office with the immigration officer.

After collecting their biometrics, Bara would be asked to stay back for the asylum interview that had been promised to him, while the rest head back to the yard.

"Hey, bro! We're leaving," said one of the Africans they had met at the camp. They had been called for release. Nothing could contain their excitement.

They stood by the room and celebrated with them until the officer sent them away.

On their way out, they met a long line of Central Americans who had been called in for deportation and release. "Amigo! Africa mafia!" they called.

"No! You mucho mafia!" the Africans responded.

They mostly communicated by jokingly accusing each other of being in the mafia. The rest of the conversation would be followed by uttering simple English words. With a combination of broken English and terrible sign language, they could sometimes drive the message across. However, it mostly left them laughing at each other and wishing the world had a common language.

An unusual population stood around the TV area on the veranda. Two camps pointed and yelled at each other, and two police officers tried as politely as they could to pacify the altercation.

A fight had started between two Indians, but it had left them divided into two camps. As the two groups stood facing each other in the presence of the security guards, one of them struggled to get loose from where he was held back by his friends.

A few spectators may have rushed to the fight scene, but the soccer match had continued carelessly.

The guards finally dismissed everyone.

"I'm shocked that these guys are fighting. They seemed so peaceful," Ali said.

Pastor replied "You know what? I feel like flexing some muscles too."

"You want to get into fight? For what reason? We really have to stop calling you pastor," Kingsley said.

Pastor said, "Come on! Not a fight. I meant this guy. I think it's time to shut him up. Who does he think he is? Call him."

Kingsley descended the stairs to alert the short, stocky Honduran guy, who had been challenging and beating everyone at arm wrestling.

It didn't take long for a crowd to gather. The Central Americans and Africans were cheering and giving their participants unsolicited advice. After checking to be sure the opponent did not have his arm in a position of advantage, they stood on opposite sides of the short wall. It ended the stairs to the right, and formed a perfect surface for the arm wrestling encounter.

Pastor had well-toned muscles and a half-grown afro. To many non-Africans, he was one of those hard-looking black men who exuded strength in everything they did. Everyone was looking forward to the encounter. Even the security guards were visibly excited.

"Three! Two! One! Go!"

The crowd began to scream.

"Pastor! Pastor! Pastor! Pastor!"

"Fernando! Fernando! Fernando! Fernando!"

They cheered in deep choruses from both sides of the short wall, and even the devoted soccer spectators and players were distracted.

Both men pushed with every drop of living strength in their blood. Fernando was truly a champion. Just like Pastor, he accompanied his clenched teeth with deep groans.

"Fernando! Fernando!" The supporters cheered even louder as he began pressing down on Pastor's hand.

Like a groaning beast, Pastor pushed back the heavy arm until they were up again in a jerky equilibrium.

"Pastor! Pastor! Pastor!" They kept cheering him on as the men stared eyeball to eyeball. Their teeth were clenched so tightly that the bones were printed out clearly on their jaws.

With another long groan to accompany the last bit of energy he had to offer, Pastor pressed down Fernando's hand in a quick jerk.

Fernando resisted. His groans grew tighter and louder. His eyes were flaming red with determination as he grappled on. His supporters chanted his name, but Fernando's strength was petering out. Slowly and steadily, his hand descended and finally landed on the slab.

Pastor had won.

In heavy breaths and friendly laughs, they shook hands over the wall.

Everyone else, including the security guards, clapped endlessly.

· · · · · · · · · ● ○○○○○○○○○ ○ ○

Pastor might have been a champion at arm wrestling—and he might have even wallowed in a sort of glory—but he wasn't talked about even half as much as the hard-faced guy by the toilet. He and a few other guys always hung around the toilet with apples—even when none had been shared in the dining hall. A straw always stuck out of the fruit.

People thought there was a substance in the fruit. They would often hide contraband in the toilet.

Sema asked, "But how is that possible when there's a security guard stationed just before the toilet. He constantly goes in there for checks?"

Pastor said, "The more disturbing question is how the substance got in here in the first place? And where do they get apples when we're given bananas or no fruits at all?"

"I guess all detainees are equal—but some are more equal than others," Ali responded. "Hey, Bara! How did it go? How was it?" Kingsley asked as Bara returned.

"It was OK, I guess. They asked me a lot of questions, and I gave them a lot of answers." He chuckled. "It took longer than I thought it would."

"Yeah, but you're just back in time for dinner," Pastor said.

Lunch had been a plate of spaghetti with two tortillas and some vegetables on the side. Most had loved it, but there had not been enough cups of juice for the Africans.

They wondered what they'd be having as they stood in line for dinner.

Kingsley said, "There is hardly enough fruit or juice for us."

Bara replied, "That's because we always eat last, but it's probably just a miscalculation because there's often a shortage for just a few people."

Kingsley said, "You're probably right. The population fluctuates a lot as people constantly come and leave the camp."

After the last Indian had just signed his name, the officer got up and took a few steps away.

Kamali concluded that the officer had been sitting for far too long and needed to stretch. He proceeded to the long white table, and Hassan and the rest followed closely behind.

The officer beat the air before his nose and covered his nostrils.

"Why is he doing that?" Kamali asked.

"Why are you blocking your nostrils, sir?" Hassan asked.

"He thinks we smell."

"Yeah!"

"That's very bad of you, sir."

The officer pointed at them and fanned his nose again.

"How racist of you!"

"You should be ashamed of yourself!"

"Racist!"

"As a matter of fact, we want to see your supervisor," Pastor demanded.

The supervisor stepped in just as Hassan began a heated altercation with the officer.

Hassan said, "Sir, this officer seems to believe that Africans are stinky. That's what he said when we came in to sign our names. We take our baths twice every day. That's more often than any other persons here. How is it possible that we're—"

"That's OK. I've heard you," the supervisor said. He took the officer and Hassan to another office, and Hassan explained what had transpired. He also explained that they had not been allowed to eat until every other race had eaten. "While we're grateful for the food, sir, it seems like we're only allowed to eat last so that if there were any shortages, then every other person would have gotten it except for us."

The supervisor said, "We feed and will continue feeding the Central Americans first because of their population. They are also our next-door neighbors—so we give them that neighborly advantage—but as far as the rest of the migrants, I greatly apologize. I will see what I can do."

"Understood, sir. Thank you very much," Hassan said.

The supervisor told the officer in candid terms to apologize or face drastic sanctions.

Hassan returned to the dining hall with the officer, and the man apologized to all the Africans.

Kingsley said, "Thanks for standing up for the rest of us, bro. I've never felt so humiliated and helpless."

Hassan replied, "Come on. You said the same thing last week when that thinning-haired woman refused to rent her hotel rooms to us."

"That's true though," Kingsley admitted.

They all laughed.

Hassan said, "Well, I hope you realize what it feels like to be discriminated against for something you haven't chosen and can't change."

"Ha! Touché," Kingsley said. "Did you see how everyone just kept eating like they didn't see what was happening to us?"

"I know, right? But what could they really have done?" Pastor replied.

CHAPTER 22

THE RAINCLOUDS HAD decided that there'd be no sun. Droplets of rain had spider-webbed the atmosphere since morning.

"Don't you prefer when it rains heavily and then stops?" Kingsley said.

Pastor said, "To be honest, I don't mind the chillness. The scorching sun has been unbearable for the past few days. And the rain is not getting anyone wet. They've been out there playing for a while, but their clothes are still dry."

It had been ten days in detention, and everything had slowly lost its cool. Soccer was still played, but the sharp sound piercing the air whenever the plastic ball bounced on the hard cement had become more of a nuisance. Even the game of coins had grown tiring, and most players had given up because they were bad at it.

At least the eating order had been addressed. There were two lists on the table by the officer in charge: one for the Africans and one for the Asians. No one would come first or last for any reason, especially because of their race or origin. Everyone got in when they got in as long as they were in line.

The loudspeaker called the Nicaraguans and Guatemalans for the fourth time.

Gilbert said, "I wonder when they'll let us out. I don't know how long I can take this place."

Hassan stood at the counter of the control room with a group of others who needed soap, deodorant, hand sanitizer, toilet paper, or toothbrushes and toothpaste.

"Hey, Hassan!" Ortega called from the line.

"Hey, guys! Are you leaving?" Hassan asked.

"Unfortunately, we are. I mean fortunately we're getting out, but it's always sad to part, especially from a good friend like you."

"Yeah. You have a very tender heart, Hassan, and for every kindness you've shown us, another will do same for you."

"Guys! Come on. That's too much flattery for me—but thank you. Damn! You guys are leaving? I'm so jealous."

They all laughed.

"Honestly, I have no idea when we'll get out of here. We probably won't see each other again, but it's been an honor to meet you both. Take care of yourselves, OK?"

"You too. Take care of yourselves, my friend," Gustavo replied.

They all hugged, and an officer escorted Hassan out of the hall.

"Did you get your asylum?" Hassan called.

"We're about to find out!"

"OK! Good luck!"

Pastor had gone to meet Kamali for soccer. He couldn't resist. He said he'd rather play the day away.

Kingsley and Gilbert joined in on the coin game.

In an hour, another crowd of migrants would arrive and revive the gloomy scene. Just as Pastor had wanted, they would play and discuss the rest of the day away.

· · · · · · · · · ● ○○○○○○○○ ○ ○

"My friend! My friend!" a guy kept calling to Kamali through the large window, which was crisscrossed with iron bars and facing the corridor in which they slept.

Kamali refused to respond. He had just fallen asleep when another voice woke him up.

"My God! Can I get some sleep?" Kamali yelled.

An officer in the middle of the corridor was reading off the names of his friends and some Asians. She ordered them to follow her with their belongings.

"Yes!" Kingsley leaped up from his bed. It was time to be released.

With smiles and uncontained excitement, they followed the officer to the dining hall. They signed documents and received a pass that gave them twenty-one days in Mexico.

"Yes! Yes! Thank God!" Bara screamed. He'd been granted asylum.

"Congratulations, bro!"

He couldn't wait to see Claudia. His joy would only be complete if she decided to apply and get hers too.

"Let's go, people!" the officer called.

They followed her to another room, identified their bags, and headed out.

The night flourished with a calming serenity, and the air was abundant and new. It massaged their starving skin with organic freshness as they rushed out through the main gate and made the camp behind them history.

A new population of migrants had arrived. They rested beneath the mango tree, anxiously waiting for their own turn to be locked up.

Bara, Sema, and Ali sat on the short roundabout that encircled the mango tree. Their eyes fixed on the blue gate they expected to open for their women at any second.

The rest had taken a taxi to town. They wanted to sleep on real beds.

Kamali had left because he would not stoop to witnessing the reunion between Ali and Emilda.

"What if she hasn't, bro?" Ali asked.

"What do you mean?" Bara asked.

"Not that I'm trying to be negative, but what if she decided not to go through with it—or if she did apply but was denied asylum? Have you considered that?"

"Don't put negative thoughts in the poor man's head," Sema said.

Bara replied, "To be honest, I don't know what I would do. I'd love for her to be happy with any decision she makes, but I don't think I could ever find another person like her."

Sema said, "Just be positive and confident, bro. Women like guys with confidence."

"Well, I guess you're right. Confidence definitely helped me with Emilda," Ali responded.

"I see! So, that is how you snatched her from Kamali?" Bara laughed.

Ali said, "We both shot our best shots, bro. Not my fault she chose me over him."

"From that reply, I can tell your beef isn't ending anytime soon," Sema said.

"It can go for as long as he wants to remain childish," Ali replied.

They waited for hours, but they were gradually caught by sleep.

"Bara. Bara. Bara."

Bara felt a gentle nudge on his arm.

"Claudia!" Bara said.

"Shut up! Who's your Claudia?"

"Damn it, Kingsley! Why am I seeing you?" Bara rubbed his sleepy eyes.

"We couldn't find a hotel," Kingsley replied.

"Why? Racism?" Bara asked.

"No. I don't think so."

Hassan said, "Yeah, not this time. I think the hotels were genuinely filled with other migrants. There were way too many people on the balconies."

"Where are the rest then?" Bara asked.

"They stayed back. They were going to keep on looking." Hassan sat next to Sema.

Bara said, "Keep your voice down. You might wake these guys up."

"I take it the girls have not been released." Kingsley used his backpack as a pillow.

"Yeah, unfortunately," Bara replied.

• • • • • • • • ● ○○○○○○○○○ ○ ○

Like a divine wonder, darkness gave way to light. The sun rose authoritatively and bathed the horizon in amber.

A gaggle of birds visited the mango tree and whistled ceaselessly as they ate the overripe fruit. *Foolish birds! Just foolish!* Bara thought. *That sound is nothing close to a lullaby.*

A toddler began crying. Perhaps, hunger had woken her up like it now did Hassan and Kinglsey.

They walked to the tap that stood at the right end of the building. After brushing their teeth, a public minibus decelerated and stopped. They couldn't believe who they saw.

"Bro!"

"What! Look at you!"

It was their friends from India, and they were ecstatic to see each other again.

"How are you, my brothers?" Sajid said.

"So good to see you again. How have you been?" Hassan replied as they exchanged hugs.

"We've been fine, brother. Thank God," Sajid replied.

"Wow! Where's Aadesh?" Kingsley asked.

Sajid said, "We left him back on the island. The wound will take some time to heal, and we couldn't wait any longer."

Hassan replied, "I see! Of course! Poor guy. Ram! Look at you, man! You almost passed out that day in the water, bro!"

They all laughed.

Sajid said, "That was nothing! You should have seen him in the jungle. That jungle is the worst place for any human being to be, bro. The things we saw!"

"I know! Well, thank God we're still here to laugh about it," Kingsley said.

They walked over to Bara.

Kingsley said, "Bara! Bara, wake up, man! You sleep a lot. Look at who we have here."

"Damn, Kingsley! You're such a nuisance." Bara dragged himself up, and he hugged his longtime Indian friends. They engaged in an animated conversation and woke everyone around them.

Two buses filled with Central Americans arrived and proceeded into the camp. The gate remained open after the second bus made its way in, and the girls rushed out.

"Finally!" Bara said as they rushed and hugged the girls.

"How was it, Solange? Do you feel all right?" Sema asked.

"Hey, babe," Ali called.

"Hey! It was tough in there," Emilda said.

"I know! But you made it. I missed you," Ali said.

Bara and Claudia remained glued together a little longer than everyone else, and Bara gave her a kiss.

"Hey, queen!" Sajid called.

Claudia screamed Sajid's name and ran into his arms.

Bara smiled, but he felt an intense urge to pull her back. While they had been together, she and Sajid had complimented each other's looks a bit too much. Sajid had been blessed with charm and looks. If it really were all about appearance, Bara would stand no chance.

"OMG, Sajid! I cannot believe this is you," she said.

"It is us," Jonte said.

They all laughed.

Claudia said, "You see!? You even learned more English! Where's Aadesh?"

"OK! Let me steal her for a moment," Bara said before she could get a reply and they both walked away toward the vehicles on the parking lot.

"Is anyone hungry?" Kingsley asked.

"As if you knew, bro! We're starving," Sajid replied.

They brushed their teeth with the haste of hungry men and caught up with each other as they walked to the restaurant, leaving Bara and Claudia behind.

• • • • • • • • ● ○○○○○○○ ○ ○ ○

Bara took Claudia by the hand. They stood behind the pickup truck that was among other vehicles in the parking lot. "Hey! I got the asylum. I'm told I can follow the process to get the rest of my documents from anywhere within the country." He smiled.

"Great! Thank God! Good for you!" Claudia said.

"No! Good for *us*, babe! You got yours too, right?" Bara did not think he could hide his disappointment if she said no. He would let her go if it made her happy—he'd promised—but he'd be broken beyond repair. He'd be crushed.

Claudia was not smiling. "Why do we seem to always find ourselves behind a vehicle?"

"Well?" Bara smiled. *God! Why is this girl playing with me?*

"Bara, your sense of fashion is despicable, and your unfamiliarity with slang and colloquialisms bores the life out of me." She moved a few steps back.

Bara's face sunk in gloom, reflecting the despair in his splitting heart.

"My grandmother once told me that most times, we find love in unexpected places and with unexpected people. Then we'll try to explain it, but there won't be a reason why. Bara, you do not meet most of my list. So, I have thought for a long time now. I promised you that I would, but I still can't explain why I feel this way about you. I just do!"

Bara smiled, but he was cautious and not overjoyed.

"Neither of us had America on our minds when we left our home country in search of safety, I know I did not. So, I won't let it get in the way of a potential happy future with you. I applied and got asylum. And, yes, I love you too, Bara!"

Bara beamed like a rising sun as he moved closer and swept her off her feet. He gave her a kiss that was so deep and real, and she trembled in passion.

"I love you more. Damn, Claudia! You scared the crap out of me. For a moment there, I thought you were going to say no." Bara was breathing like he had just run a marathon. "OK, let me quickly brush my teeth, and then we'll join the others for breakfast."

"You haven't brushed your teeth yet? No way!"

They laughed endlessly.

"Nasty! Ew!" she joked as they left for the restaurant.

They would have loved to be the first to announce that they were now together officially, but they'd been the topic of discussion—and Linda had already told the guys that Claudia was all in.

Kofi and Hendry had taken the bus from town to get plantains and chicken. They also had to tell their friends about the hotel they had found with Pastor, Kamali, and Gilbert. They had now just finished eating with the others.

"Oh my God! Sajid, I'm going to miss you!" Claudia said as they hugged the Indians.

"I'll miss you more, queen," Sajid replied.

"Remember to stay connected on Facebook, bro," Kingsley shouted.

They hurriedly got on another bus, and it drove away to the hotel, where they all slumbered through the better half of the day.

That evening, they would purchase bus tickets for their next destination.

CHAPTER 23

THERE WERE NO early walkers or joggers—Tapachula was not that sort of place—but school buses and public buses crisscrossed the city. White-collar workers waited by the classic roadside restaurants that had begun serving coffee.

At the bus terminal, Bara and Claudia stood to say goodbye.

Claudia said, "I'm not going to cry—I promise." She hugged everyone.

Kingsley said, "Bro, are you sure you haven't changed your mind and want to come with us?"

"God knows I cannot deal with the confinement of another immigration camp," Bara replied.

"I guess you're really doing this. Well, all the best, brother. Looks like you have it all figured out," Kingsley said.

"Wish you the best too, my brother, but I honestly don't have it all figured out. Just trusting my gut," Bara said.

A general mood of melancholy reigned in their hearts. They had been through so much together. They had laughed and cried, fought, lost and won, all together. Standing there now—not willing to part but having to, anyway—was sad. They had formed strong friendships, and what mattered? They would probably shatter if they depended on the passiveness of Facebook.

Hassan said, "Why must we always part? Why is life so momentary? Especially the good things in it?"

Claudia said, "Hassan, please! I'm trying to fight back these tears. Pastor, I'd probably not be here if not for you." She finally released a tear.

"Hey! Come on. Don't do that. You're OK now—and that's all that matters. No more nightmares and definitely no more memories of that event, OK? Take care of yourself, sweetheart." Pastor released the hug as the bus sounded its horn.

"OK, dear, be well," Solange said.

"I will, sweetheart. You too. And name that beautiful baby after me," Claudia said.

"Ha! I just might," Solange replied.

"Stay connected please!"

"Wish you all the best, bro."

They quickly gave their last hugs and rushed onboard.

"Whoever put the good in goodbye was out of their mind," Claudia said.

They waved as their friends disappeared with the vehicle.

"So, what do you have in mind for today?" Bara asked.

"Please let's start by visiting that shop. I need lipstick. I have to revive myself—please!" Claudia said.

It was true that they did not have it all figured out. Even as they sat in the taxi, returning to their hotel, where they would prepare for their trip to Mexico City the next day, they still had no idea how they would handle a police encounter. They didn't speak Spanish, and who knew if the police there, would be patient with foreigners. God forbid they encounter the wrong ones. A kind immigration officer in Tapachula had contacted an NGO that promised to receive and help them, but they still had no clue how the rest of the city would react to foreigners. Still, they were determined to go. They were determined to help each other realize their dreams and be happy together.

For four days, all they did was sleep and stop at roadside diners to eat and use the bathroom.

The highway meandered across undulating hills, and the night spread its black wings and unloaded a darkness across the horizon.

A mile or two later, a vista of city lights burst through the stagnant darkness. It sparkled like stars on earth.

"Welcome to Tijuana," the driver announced as he parked.

"Such a beautiful city. Absolutely stunning."

Unlike Tapachula, it would be quite easy to find a hotel. The cost would be a little higher, but for such a winsome city, every penny asked was deserved. Like Tapachula, the hotels operated under the same strictures of no noise and no unauthorized visitors.

Tijuana was bitingly cold, but the impeccable infrastructure, the classic frenzy, and the jovial people were a balm to their hearts. They spent a week in the city.

"Someone has to recognize this city for its dedication to health," Hassan said.

"Why do you say that?" Pastor asked.

"Just observe. Every block stands with a functioning pharmacy," Hassan replied.

"For real!" Kingsley said.

They were headed to immigration in taxis with the cards they'd received in Tapachula.

Two immigration officers sat under a canopy that backed the busy road. Hundreds of migrants were waiting anxiously for their names to be called. TV channels and NGOs were interviewing migrants and collecting data.

Pastor said, "One would think from watching the news that only Africans and Central Americans are desperately running away from their countries." Scanning the crowd, he saw Asians and Europeans also seeking refuge in the United States of America.

The officers began calling numbers and names and gathering everyone who answered. As usual, everyone was expecting an exceptional day, but only fifteen numbers were called per day. That morning was no different.

"I don't know how I feel," Kingsley said. They'd been lucky to be among the chosen ones that morning. They sat in a little bus that would transport them to the American immigration authorities.

"How do you feel?" Solange asked, struggling for comfort with her significantly protruding belly.

Kingsley said, "My whole life, I heard about America. I watched their movies and even learned a little about the country in Human and Economic Geography Class. Fishing off the coast of Alaska sounded fascinating. America sounded so distant geographically and out of reach in every other way. I am about to step on that soil in a matter of minutes, and I can't tell how I feel,"

They mostly agreed with him and admitted that the closer they got to the border, the more conflicting it felt. It felt like they were heading to a place that was both enchanting and dreadful. A place, everlastingly peaceful and violent all at once. It had a powerful, harmonious energy, but it was polarized by endless discord. A place like every other—but like no other.

The bus stopped at the border. A group of border police was scanning every vehicle coming in from Mexico. An officer led them through a tiny gate and straight into the building. They didn't have enough time to appreciate the exterior—not that they wanted to.

"Line up here!" a muscular woman said.

"English, finally! Thank God! Hassan, I no longer need you for translation," Kingsley said.

They all began to laugh.

"Quiet!" the lady ordered.

This immigration center was different, and the earlier they knew that, the better it would be for them all.

They went to the counter and registered their names and nationalities. They were ordered to take off their shoelaces and undershirts. They would only be allowed to have a T-shirt and a sweater.

Another officer distributed cards, and they wrote their names and countries as instructed. He clipped them to each of the bags and took them away. It would be the last time they'd see the bags for a long while.

"This way!" The lady pointed to all the females.

When she returned for the males, they followed to the elevator.

In a hypnotizing melody, a brilliant African artist once sang, "Don't lose what you've got / For what you don't know / For the grass isn't always greener on the other side."

For some reason, the lyric kept replaying in Kingsley's head as the packed elevator descended three floors. It finally burped them out into a windowless basement. No matter how much it glittered, it exuded a dark uncertainty that was intensified when an officer walked in. On his slate board, a single word was printed in bold ink: "Trauma."

STILL TO COME

A RUTHLESS CHILL SEIZED the narrow corridors. Jingles of dangling chains and cuffs afflicted the ears as the officers paraded to and fro, dishing out stern orders.

"Legs open and faces to the wall!"

It was not obligatory, but most chose to close their eyes as the cold metal gripped their legs from behind. They turned on demand and received chains around their waists. They were fastened and linked to the cuffs that locked their arms.

"Move! Let's go!"

They started the long and uneasy walk through the dark hallways. What had they gotten themselves into?

ABOUT THE AUTHOR

DEMIAN WIYSAHNYUY (DEMIAN. W)** was born, raised and educated in West Cameroon. He finally graduated with a Bachelor of Science in Mining and Extractive Metallurgy from the Cameroon Christian University Institute in 2016. His intentions are to use any agency necessary, be it through music, books and film, to tell stories that have direct impacts on society. Demian moved to the United States, escaping the conflict that led his country into the unfortunate war, that has now been known by the world as the 'Anglophone Crises'. It was during his time in the U.S asylum detention camps and his interaction with countless other asylum seekers, that he began writing what will become his first ever published book, 'WHEN HOME FAILS'.

Printed in the United States
by Baker & Taylor Publisher Services